The Broken Circle

Mending Loss Through Memories

Rene' Stanley

Rene' Stanley

Contents

1. Chapter 1 — 1

2. Chapter 2 — 12

3. Chapter 3 — 23

4. Chapter 4 — 35

5. Chapter 5 — 48

6. Chapter 6 — 60

7. Chapter 7 — 72

8. Chapter 8 — 84

9. Chapter 9 — 96

10. Chapter 10 — 109

Afterword — 121

About the author — 123

CHAPTER ONE

Dear Daddy,

Today marks five years since you passed. Five years since I last heard your deep, rumbling laugh shake the room like summer thunder. Five years of wanting to pick up the phone and dial the number etched into my fingers, my heart.

I still remember that night, Daddy. The phone ringing, Mama's choked sobs from the kitchen, the linoleum cold against my bare feet as I sprinted for the receiver. "Daddy had an accident," she said, eyes swollen. "He's gone home to be with the Lord." Just like that, my world shattered into a million jagged pieces.

At seventeen, I thought I knew heartbreak. The boy with hazel eyes and empty promises. The C- in Chemistry that ended my honor roll streak. Petty disappointments that barely scratched the surface. But this.

Losing you. I didn't know a heart could break this deeply, this completely.

They say grief comes in stages. Denial. Anger. Bargaining. Depression. Acceptance. But they don't mention how the stages tangle together, a twisted mess of emotions without beginning or end. They don't tell you how one moment you're numb, and the next, the pain steals your breath.

I keep the photo from my tenth birthday in my wallet. You, tall and proud in your crisp Navy uniform. Me, gap-toothed, pigtails askew, giggling as I blow out the candles. Your arm around Mama's waist. Both of you beaming like I had plucked the moon from the sky by simply turning double digits. What I wouldn't give for one more birthday like that.

I still talk to you, Daddy. When the ache in my chest threatens to swallow me whole, I close my eyes and imagine you next to me, your sage advice a balm to my worried mind. "Have faith, baby girl," you'd say. "God didn't bring you this far to let you fall." I cling to those words when the world feels too heavy, too harsh.

High school isn't the same without you cheering me on at track meets, without your bear hugs after a hard day. The college brochures piling up on my desk fill me with equal parts excitement and dread. How can I take this next step without you to guide me, to catch me if I stumble?

But I hear your voice, Daddy. "Spread your wings, Remi. This world has a grand adventure waiting just for you." So I take a deep breath, square my shoulders. I pray for an ounce of your courage, your unwavering faith.

The road ahead seems daunting, uncertain. But I carry you with me. Your strength, your wisdom, your unconditional love. The legacy of a man who taught me to face each day with a grateful heart and a fierce determination.

I love you, Daddy. I miss you. Until we meet again.

Your baby girl,

Remi

***

The hardwood floor creaks beneath my feet as I pace my bedroom, memories flooding my mind. Saturdays with you, Daddy. Our weekly pilgrimage to Grandma Rose's tidy brick bungalow across town.

I loved those mornings. Waking at dawn, the air thick with the aroma of Mama's pecan waffles. You, humming a Marvin Gaye tune, off-key and joyful. "Rise and shine, baby girl!" you'd call. "Adventure awaits!"

Hand in hand, we'd walk the tree-lined streets, you matching your long strides to my eager skips. The journey was as much a treat as the destination. You'd point out the robins nesting in the maple trees, pause to admire Miss Ella's vibrant tulips. Every detail a wonder through your eyes.

At the corner of Sycamore and Vine, we'd stop at Mr. Jameson's newsstand. "Well, if it isn't the dynamic duo!" he'd boom, his weathered face crinkling into a smile. He'd wink, slip me a strawberry Jolly Rancher, and ask about school. You and Mr. Jameson would chat, swapping stories of your Navy days, while I studied the comic book covers, dreaming of superpowers.

Six blocks and countless stories later, we'd reach the porch steps, the sweet scent of gardenias welcoming us. Grandma Rose, arms outstretched, waited at the door. "There's my sunshine!" she'd say, folding me into her soft embrace.

Those Saturdays sparkled with laughter, love, and the magic of being wholly, unconditionally cherished. The hours melted like butter on Grandma Rose's famous yeast rolls as we pored over photo albums, you and Grandma recounting family lore. The mischief you and Uncle Isaac caused as boys. The day you met Mama at the church picnic, how you knew in an instant she was your soulmate.

I soaked up every tale, every scrap of family history. Those stories, Daddy, knit me to a legacy stretching back generations. A patchwork heritage of resilience, faith, and unshakable love.

In Grandma's sunlit kitchen, you'd teach me to play Spades, your rich baritone weaving life lessons between hands. "Pay attention to the cards played, Remi. In Spades and in life, you've got to be strategic. Think three moves ahead."

I held those pearls of wisdom close, tucked next to my heart. Even now, when life deals me a tough hand, I hear your voice. Patience. Faith. Keep moving forward. The gifts you gave me, Daddy, continue to light my path.

As shadows lengthened and the day drew to a close, you'd scoop me up, drowsy and contented. "Let's get you home to Mama, baby girl." On the walk back, the neighborhood buzzing with crickets and porch chatter, I'd lean my head against your sturdy shoulder. The safest place in the world.

I'd give anything for one more Saturday, Daddy. One more walk, one more story, one more game of Spades. But I hold tight to the memories, the lessons. Though I navigate this world without your hand to hold, your love still guides me. In every step, every choice, every triumph, and every setback, you are with me.

In memory and love,

Remi

***

Daddy,

Junior year is kicking my butt. Pre-calc, AP English, SAT prep—my planner looks like a war zone of highlighter and post-its. Some days, I want to crawl back into kindergarten, when the biggest challenge was remembering to wash my hands after finger painting.

Remember how you'd sit with me before big tests? We'd sip hot chocolate, extra marshmallows, while you quizzed me on vocab words and equations. "You've got this, Remi," you'd say, your certainty a tangible force. "You're the smartest cookie I know."

I could use one of those pep talks now, Daddy. The pressure feels suffocating sometimes. Mama does her best, but it's not the same. She looks at me with such hope, such expectation. "You're going to do great things, baby," she says, her eyes misty. "Make your daddy proud." As if I could ever measure up to the man you were.

Mr. Jackson, my English teacher, pulled me aside after class last week. "Remi, I was looking over your college essay," he said, tapping the pages on his desk. "The way you write about your father... it's powerful. Raw. I felt like I knew him by the end."

I ducked my head, embarrassed and pleased. Writing is the one place I feel close to you, Daddy. When the words flow, it's like you're right beside me, nudging me along.

Mr. Jackson leaned forward, his expression earnest. "Have you considered applying to HBCUs? I think you'd thrive in that environment, Remi. A place where you can explore your identity, your heritage, surrounded by a supportive community."

HBCUs. Historically Black Colleges and Universities. The thought had crossed my mind, but I'd pushed it aside. Mama talks about me staying close to home, commuting to the state school 30 minutes away. "I need you nearby," she says, her smile tight. "We've got to stick together."

But Mr. Jackson's words lit a spark, Daddy. The idea of stepping out on my own, discovering who I am apart from the roles of daughter, sister, student. Of honoring our history, our culture, in a space created just for us. Is it selfish to want that?

I know you'd tell me to chase my dreams, to trust in God's plan. "He's already written your story, Remi," you'd say, your hand warm on my shoulder. "Walk in faith, not fear."

I'm trying, Daddy. I'm trying to be brave, to picture a future that both excites and terrifies me. A future without you in it.

Late at night, when doubts swirl like shadows, I think of all the times you whispered, "Déu apò tou"—our little secret. The Yoruba words you taught me, passed down from Grandma Rose. "God is with you." A talisman against the dark.

I hold those words close as I navigate this labyrinth of growing up. When I falter, I remember the strength of your embrace, the conviction in your eyes. The little girl who thought her daddy hung the moon is learning to find that light within herself.

Watch over me.

Love,

Remi

***

Daddy,

I dreamed of you last night. We were on the beach, the one where you taught me to swim. Salt on my tongue, sun on my back. You were laughing, head thrown back, as you splashed in the surf.

"Look at you, baby girl," you called over the roar of the waves. "An adventurer, just like your old man!"

I woke with the ghost of your voice in my ears. Even now, memories of you weave through my days. A song on the radio, a whiff of Old Spice, the glint of dog tags. Little reminders that even though you're gone, you're never far.

Those tags. I remember the day you explained what they meant. "These aren't just hunks of metal, Remi," you said, your fingers curled around the chain at your neck. "They're a symbol. Of duty. Sacrifice. Brotherhood."

You told me stories, your eyes distant. Late nights on the ship, the ocean an inky expanse. The camaraderie of your fellow sailors, the shared purpose. The times you were afraid but pushed through.

"In the face of fear, we find our true strength," you said. The words resonated, a tuning fork to my soul.

I think of your service often, Daddy. The way you and your brothers—Uncle Isaac in the Air Force, Uncle Jeremiah and Uncle Caleb in the Army—dedicated your lives to something greater than yourselves. Whenever I saw you in your dress whites, ribbons and medals gleaming, my heart nearly burst with pride.

That legacy of service, of courage in the face of adversity... it's woven into my DNA. Marrow deep, soul deep. And now, as I stand on the cusp of adulthood, I feel that same call. A tug toward a life of purpose.

Mama frets when I mention enlisting, her hands fluttering like startled birds. "It's too dangerous," she says. "I can't lose you too." My heart aches for her, for the fear she carries. But I know you'd understand, Daddy. The desire to be part of something bigger, to push my limits.

I haven't made any decisions yet. There's still time. But I carry your spirit with me as I wrestle with the future. Your bravery, your integrity, your unwavering faith—they are my North Star.

In quiet moments, I imagine the advice you'd give. "Pray on it, Remi," you'd say. "Listen to your heart and trust the path God lays before you. And remember, no matter what you choose, I'm proud of you. Always."

Your pride, your love... they are my armor. My compass. The knowledge that whatever I decide, you'll be right beside me—if not in body, then in spirit.

"Déu apò tou," I whisper to the dark. God is with me. And so are you, Daddy.

Until I see you again, in dreams and memories.

Ọmọ rẹ (your child),

Remi

CHAPTER TWO

Dear Daddy,

Prom season is in full swing and the halls are buzzing with dress gossip and promposal plans. Girls gush over sequins and tulle while boys mumble about tux rentals. Me? I'm bracing myself for an onslaught of cheesy pickup lines and halfhearted invitations.

It's not that I don't want to go. A night of dressing up, dancing with friends, making memories—it sounds fun. But the whole dating scene feels like navigating a minefield. Especially without your guidance.

I remember our talk, the summer before high school. We were tinkering with the Chevy, a smudge of grease on your chin. "Boys are going to start noticing you, Remi," you said, your eyes crinkling. "And who could blame them? But you've got to set standards. Know your worth."

You made it sound so simple. "Don't settle for anyone who doesn't respect you, who doesn't support your dreams. Find someone who looks at you the way I look at your mama. Like you hung the moon and stars."

I nodded, folding your words into my heart. But Daddy, it's not easy. The boys at school, they're all swagger and bravado. They toss around compliments like candy wrappers, all flash and no substance.

Take Jayden, the point guard on the basketball team. Last week, he cornered me by my locker, all sly smiles. "Remi, you're looking fly today. How about you let me take you out sometime?"

I wanted to roll my eyes. Jayden, who's left a trail of broken hearts behind him. Who cheats on tests and brags about it. I thought of your unwavering integrity, the way you treated Mama like a queen.

"Thanks, but no thanks," I said, my chin high. "I'm focusing on my studies right now." He shrugged, unfazed, and sauntered off to his next target.

I wish I could talk to you about this, Daddy. Sift through the noise and nonsense with your steady wisdom. You'd probably chuckle, shake your head. "Teenage boys, they've got a lot of growing to do. Don't be in a rush, baby girl. The right one will come along when the time is right."

I'm holding out for that, Daddy. For someone who shares my values, my faith. Someone who will walk beside me, not try to lead me astray. Someone who looks at me and sees a partner, an equal. The way you saw Mama.

In the meantime, I've got my girls. Zuri, Amara, Imani—my ride-or-dies. We're planning a pre-prom sleepover, a night of facemasks and rom-coms and boy-talk. A little slice of normalcy in this whirlwind of hormones and expectations.

And who knows? Maybe I'll go stag to prom, dance the night away with my head held high. Or maybe, by some miracle, a diamond in the rough will emerge. A boy who remembers the lessons his daddy taught him, just like I remember yours.

Either way, I carry your love with me. My armor, my compass. Guiding me through this crazy labyrinth of growing up.

I'll make you proud, Daddy. My moon and stars.

Love always,

Daddy,

Remember those nights, curled up on the couch, a tattered copy of "Anansi the Spider" balanced on your knee? Your rich baritone breathed life into the trickster's tales, your hands casting shadows on the wall. I'd nestle into your side, transfixed, as you spun stories of cleverness, courage, and the power of wit over might.

Those were the moments I felt the magic of our heritage, the threads that tied us to generations past. The same stories Grandma Rose told you, her daddy told her, stretching back and back, a tapestry of wisdom and wonder.

I think about those tales now, as I navigate the tangled web of high school. The cliques, the drama, the constant jockeying for status. It's easy to get caught up in it all, to forget what really matters.

But then I remember Anansi, outsmarting the larger animals, using his brain to overcome obstacles. And I hear your voice, a steady compass: "Remi, you've got a good head on your shoulders. Don't let anyone make you forget that."

It's not always easy, Daddy. Sometimes I feel like the odd one out, the girl who'd rather spend her free period in the library than gossiping in the hallways. The one who speaks up in class, even when it means risking eye rolls and snickers.

Like last week, in history. We were discussing the Civil Rights Movement, and Mr. Thompson mentioned the March on Washington. Hands shot up, students eager to show they knew about Dr. King's "I Have a Dream" speech.

But then Ty, lounging in the back row, mumbled, "Yeah, and look how much good that did. Racism's still alive and well."

The room fell silent, heavy with discomfort. Mr. Thompson cleared his throat, ready to move on. But something in me bristled.

I raised my hand, heart pounding. "Yes, racism is still a problem. But that doesn't negate the progress made by Dr. King and so many others. They paved the way for us to keep fighting, to keep dreaming. We can't let cynicism win."

Ty shrugged, but a few classmates nodded. Mr. Thompson smiled, a glimmer of pride in his eyes.

I thought of you, Daddy. The way you always stood up for what was right, even when it was hard. The way you taught me to be proud of our history, our identity.

"Baby girl," you'd say, "you come from a long line of dreamers and doers. Never forget that. Your voice matters."

I carry that with me, Daddy. In the classroom, in the hallways, in the quiet of my own heart. When I feel lost or small, I summon the strength of our stories, our legacy.

And on the days when I miss you most, when the ache of your absence feels like a physical thing, I pull out my dog-eared copy of "Anansi the Spider." I trace the familiar illustrations, hear the echo of your voice in the worn pages.

In those moments, I am that little girl again, safe in the circle of your arms. Learning, through the wisdom of those tales, how to spin my own story. One of resilience, hope, and the quiet power of staying true to myself.

Thank you for those gifts, Daddy. For the stories, the lessons, the love. I carry them with me, always.

Your little dreamer,

Remi

***

Dear Daddy,

The kitchen table is buried beneath a mountain of college brochures, each one glossier than the last.

Smiling students lounge on manicured quads, their futures bright and shiny as pennies. Meanwhile, I'm drowning in a sea of application deadlines and essay prompts.

I wish you were here to help me navigate this, Daddy. To sift through the marketing jargon and find the schools that fit me best. You always saw through the fluff, straight to the heart of things.

Mama tries, bless her. She's taken off work to drive me to campus tours, her voice bright with forced cheer. But I see the worry in the furrow of her brow, the way her fingers clench the steering wheel.

For her, college is a ticket to a life she never had. A way to secure my future in a world that's not always kind to girls like me. "Education is freedom, Remi," she says, her eyes fierce. "No one can take it from you."

I know she's right. But Daddy, sometimes the weight of her expectations feels like a yoke around my neck. Like my dreams are too small, too fragile to voice aloud.

Remember when I was seven, determined to be an astronaut? You bought me that telescope for Christmas, taught me to map the constellations. "Shoot for the moon, baby girl," you said. "Even if you miss, you'll land among the stars."

I clung to that, the permission to dream big. But now, with the realities of tuition and job prospects looming, my aspirations feel childish. Foolish, even.

The career counselor at school, Mrs. Winters, she means well. But her suggestions feel like ill-fitting shoes. "With your grades, Remi, you'd make an excellent engineer. Or a doctor, perhaps. Something stable, with good earning potential."

I nod, force a smile. But inside, I'm wilting. Where is the passion in that? The joy? I think of your workshop, Daddy. The hours you'd spend hunched over a sketch pad, lost in a world of your own making. The way your face would light up as you showed me your latest creation, your hands bringing beauty to life.

That's what I want. To wake up each day excited to pour my heart into something I love. Something that feeds my soul, not just my bank account. Is that naive? Selfish, even, with Mama counting on me?

Late at night, my mind spinning, I pray. For guidance, for clarity. And in the stillness, I hear your voice. "Remi, my love. Your gifts are just that—gifts. Meant to be shared, not squandered. Trust your heart, and the rest will follow."

I'm trying, Daddy. To hold onto that trust, that faith. To picture a future that marries practicality with passion.

It's not easy, this business of growing up. Of shoulder-ing the weight of so many hopes and dreams.

But I carry you with me, always. Your belief, your en-couragement. The certainty that wherever this wind-ing path leads, you'll be cheering me on. My North Star, steady and true.

Watch over me, Daddy. Light my way.

Your little dreamer,

Remi

***

Daddy,

It's 2am and sleep eludes me, chased away by the whirring of my mind. The college question looms large, a shadow I can't shake.

I've been praying, seeking guidance. Asking God to lead me toward the path He's chosen. But in the quiet of my room, it's your voice I long for. Your steadying presence, your unwavering faith.

I think back to the night of my baptism. Twelve years old, my heart thrumming with a mixture of nerves and joy. You stood beside me in the sanctuary, your hand on my shoulder.

"Today, you're making the most important decision of your life," you said, your eyes shining. "Giving your life to Christ. No matter what comes, He will be your rock. Your refuge."

I felt it then, the weight and wonder of that commitment. The assurance that I was never alone, never without hope.

You lived that truth, Daddy. In the way you loved, the way you served. The way you faced trials with a steadiness that could only come from deep roots.

When the factory closed and money was tight, you held fast to your faith. "God will provide," you told Mama, holding her close. And He did. Through odd jobs and answered prayers, through the generosity of friends and strangers.

You taught me to trust in His plan, even when I couldn't see the road ahead. "He's writing your story, Remi," you'd say. "Each chapter, each verse. Trust the Author."

I'm clinging to that now, as I wrestle with this decision. The brochures, the applications, they're just pieces of the puzzle. It's the still, small voice I'm straining to hear. The whisper of purpose, of calling.

I think of the verses we'd recite together, huddled over my Bible. Jeremiah 29:11, a balm to my anxious heart.

"For I know the plans I have for you, declares the Lord. Plans to prosper you and not to harm you, plans to give you hope and a future."

That's the promise I hold onto, Daddy. The belief that my story, my future, is held in hands far more capable than my own. That each step, each decision, is a thread in a tapestry I can only glimpse in part.

So I'll keep seeking, keep listening. Trusting that the same God who brought me this far will lead me onward. And on the nights when doubt creeps in, when the path seems shrouded in shadow, I'll remember your words.

"Faith isn't about having all the answers, baby girl. It's about trusting the One who does."

In that trust, I find peace. The assurance that whatever lies ahead, I carry your love, your legacy, with me. A light to guide me, a foundation to steady me.

Thank you, Daddy. For the gift of your faith, your wisdom. For showing me how to walk this journey with eyes fixed on things above.

I love you. I miss you. But I know you're never far.

Your little prayer warrior,

Remi

CHAPTER THREE

Dear Daddy,

The envelope in my hands feels weighted, momentous. The Georgetown University crest gleams against the ivory paper, a herald of futures yet unwritten.

With trembling fingers, I slide the letter from its confines. The words blur before my eyes, anticipation a living thing in my chest. And then, like the sun breaking through clouds, four words illuminate the page: "We are pleased to offer you admission..."

A gasp escapes my lips, morphing into a laugh, a sob. Mama's there in an instant, her arms crushing me to her chest. "You did it, baby," she whispers, her tears mingling with mine. "You did it."

I want to shout it from the rooftops, Daddy. To share this moment with you. I can picture your face, the way your eyes would crinkle at the corners, your smile brighter than a thousand suns. "That's my girl," you'd say, your voice hoarse with pride. "My little world-changer."

Georgetown. The school of your dreams, the one you whispered about as you pored over my homework, quizzed me on vocab words. The place you saw as a launchpad for your brilliant daughter, your legacy.

But more than that, Daddy, it's a promise. To myself, to you. To honor the sacrifices you made, the love you poured into me. To take the gifts you nurtured and use them to make a difference, to be a light in the darkness.

I think of our talks, the way you'd lean against my doorframe, your eyes soft. "Remi, my love. You've got a mind like a steel trap and a heart big as the ocean. Don't you ever let anyone tell you what you can't do. You hear me?"

I heard you, Daddy. Even when the doubts crept in, when the path seemed steep and riddled with brambles. Your voice was my compass, your belief a lit torch guiding me home.

Georgetown won't be easy. A new city, new challenges. But I carry you with me, always. Your strength, your resilience, your unshakable faith. The lessons you taught without ever cracking a textbook.

Like the time you found me crying over a cruel comment, some careless words slung by a classmate. You knelt before me, your hands gentle on my shoulders.

"Baby girl, listen to me. You are fearfully and wonderfully made, crafted in the very image of God. No one can dim the light that shines from within you. Wear it proud, like a crown."

I will, Daddy. At Georgetown and beyond. I'll wear my identity like a badge of honor, a testament to the rich soil from which I've grown. The love, the legacy, the prayers that have carried me.

As I prepare to step into this new chapter, I feel you close. My silent cheering section, my most steadfast supporter. The one who saw the best in me, even when I stumbled.

Thank you, Daddy. For the gift of this moment, this opportunity. For the roots you gave me and the wings you helped me grow. I'll make you proud. Not just with degrees and accolades, but with a life poured out in service, in love.

Watch over me as I take this leap. And save me a dance when I cross that stage, diploma in hand. It'll be for you, Daddy. Always for you.

Your Georgetown Girl,

Remi

***

Daddy,

Amidst the flurry of admissions letters and congrat-
ulatory hugs, my mind keeps drifting back to those
sun-dappled afternoons in your workshop. The scent
of linseed oil and turpentine, the soft scratching of
charcoal against paper.

Those were the hours I felt most alive, most seen.
When the world beyond the garage walls fell away and
it was just you, me, and the blank canvas before us.

You'd stand behind me, your hand gentle on my
shoulder. "Close your eyes, Remi," you'd say, your
voice a low rumble. "Breathe deep. What do you feel?
What story wants to be told?"

And I would. Eyes shut, heart open. Letting the feelings
flow from my core, down my arm, through my fingertips. Charcoal, then paint, giving form to the formless.
Abstracting the inexpressible.

You taught me to see beauty in the ordinary, Daddy.
To find the magic in the mundane. A rusted coffee can
became a study in texture and shadow. A forgotten
shoe, a meditation on absence and presence.

"Art is about more than just pretty pictures, baby girl," you'd say, your eyes crinkling. "It's about truth-telling. About shining a light in the dark corners, revealing what's hidden."

I carried those lessons with me, even when the canvas lay fallow. Through the late nights hunched over textbooks, the early mornings spent pounding the track. Your words were a steady heartbeat, a reminder of the power I held.

When the Georgetown acceptance letter arrived, a part of me quaked. The practical side, the one drilled in SAT strategies and college rankings. What about my art? What if, in the pursuit of academic excellence, I let that piece of myself wither?

But then, like a gentle hand on my shoulder, I felt your presence. Your assurance. "Remi, my love. Your art isn't separate from the rest of you. It is you. The way you see, the way you feel. Don't you ever let that go."

I won't, Daddy. I promise. Even as I step into this new world of lecture halls and libraries, I'll carry my sketchbook. My charcoals, my paints. The tools of my truth-telling.

I'll find beauty in the ivy-draped buildings, the faces of my classmates. I'll let my art be my anchor, my refuge. A way to process the challenges and triumphs, the long nights and longer days.

And when doubt creeps in, when I feel the tug of comparison and conformity, I'll close my eyes. Breathe deep. Remember those golden hours in your workshop, the smell of creation thick in the air.

I'll hear your voice, a steady whisper. "Keep shining, baby girl. Keep telling your truth. The world needs your light, your story."

I will, Daddy. With every sketch, every stroke of the brush. I'll honor the gift you nurtured, the spark you fanned to flame.

And someday, when my dorm room walls are covered in canvases, when the paint stains my fingertips like badges of honor, I'll think of you. My first teacher, my most ardent supporter.

Thank you, Daddy. For seeing the artist in me, even when I was too young to hold a brush. For giving me a language beyond words, a way to make sense of the world.

I'll make you proud. In the studio and beyond. A lifetime of truth-telling, of light-shining. All because of you.

Your little artist,
Remi

***

Dear Daddy,

Today, I watched the sun set over our little town for the last time as a resident. Tomorrow, I'll wake in the blue-gray light of dawn and load the last of my boxes into Mama's car. We'll make the long drive to D.C., to the storied halls of Georgetown and the unknowns of my future.

I'm excited, of course. Giddy with the promise of new faces, new places. But beneath the thrill hums an ache, a pulsing awareness of what I'm leaving behind.

It's not just the house, with its creaking floorboards and porch swing. Or the town, with its quaint Main Street and Friday night football games. It's something deeper, more elemental.

It's the way Mama bustles around the kitchen, her worry a palpable thing. The way she lingers in my doorway at night, her eyes mapping my face like she's committing it to memory.

"My baby," she murmurs, her hand soft on my cheek. "All grown up and ready to fly."

I lean into her touch, breathing in the scent of her lavender lotion. The scent of home, of comfort. "I'll always come back to you," I promise, my throat thick. "No matter how far I go."

She smiles then, a wobbly thing. "I know, baby. But it's okay to spread your wings, too. To chase those big dreams of yours. Just don't forget your roots, yeah?"

I nod, blinking back tears. How could I forget? This place, these people, they're woven into my DNA. The rich soil from which I've grown.

I think of my brothers, all gangly limbs and goofy grins. The way they've looked up to me, their big sister with the big plans. "You're gonna kill it at Georgetown, Rem," they say, their eyes shining. "Show 'em what us Johnsons are made of."

I ruffle their hair, pull them in close. My little partners in crime, my constant reminders to stay playful, to find joy in the journey. "You know it," I say, my grin matching theirs. "And you two? You're gonna make me proud. Keep hitting those books, you hear?"

They nod, all earnest energy. And I'm struck by how much they've grown, how the years have turned them from chubby-cheeked toddlers to young men on the cusp of their own adventures.

Was this how you felt, Daddy? Watching me stretch and reach, knowing that each day brought me closer to a world beyond your watchful gaze? Did your heart swell with pride even as it ached with the bittersweet knowledge that I was yours to love but not to keep?

I wish I could ask you. Wish I could curl into the crook of your arm and spill my fears, my hopes. Feel your rumbling assurance that this next step is just another page in the story you always knew I'd write.

But even in your absence, I feel you near. Your love, your lessons, an invisible cloak draped over my shoulders. As I zip up my suitcase and take one last sweeping look at my childhood bedroom, I know I carry you with me.

"Déu apò tou," I whisper, a benediction and a balm.

Tomorrow, the road will unfurl before me. A ribbon of promise, of possibility. And with each mile marker, I'll feel your hand in mine. Your strength, your certainty.

I love you, Daddy. I miss you. And I'll make you proud. Watch over me.

Your little girl, all grown up,
Remi

Daddy,

The car is packed, the tank full. In a few short hours, I'll be on my way to Georgetown, to the next chapter of my life. But before I go, there's one more thing I need to do.

I make my way to the backyard, to the old oak tree that's stood sentry over our family for generations. Its gnarled branches reach skyward, a testament to resilience, to weathering storms and standing tall.

Nestled between its roots lies a small wooden box, weathered with age. I kneel, my fingers tracing the rough edges. Slowly, reverently, I lift the lid.

Inside, a treasure trove of memories. A cigar box, like the ones Grandpa Joe used to keep on his mantle. A Blues Alley matchbook, a reminder of Tia Rosa's singing days. And a dog tag, edges worn smooth from years of worrying fingers.

Yours, Daddy. The one you wore close to your heart, a talisman and a testament. I lift it from the box, the metal warm against my palm.

"Déu apò tou," I whisper, the Yoruba sliding from my tongue like a prayer. God is with you.

I think of all the times I saw you rub this tag, your eyes distant. The times you'd catch my questioning gaze and smile, soft and slow. "Just reminding myself what matters, baby girl," you'd say. "Faith. Family. Love."

I loop the tag around my neck, the weight of it a comfort, an anchor. A piece of you to carry close, a reminder of the man who taught me how to stand tall, how to weather storms.

As I rise, I feel a hand on my shoulder. Mama. Her eyes are misty, her smile tremulous. "He'd be so proud of you," she says, her voice a whisper. "So proud of the woman you've become."

I lean into her, breathing in her strength, her softness. "I couldn't have done it without him," I murmur. "Without both of you."

We stand there a moment, a tableau of grief and gratitude. The oak rustles above us, a benediction and a balm.

And then, with a deep breath, I turn toward the house. Toward the car that will carry me to new horizons, new adventures. My brothers wait on the porch, all long limbs and lopsided grins.

"You ready, college girl?" they call, their voices a mix of mirth and melancholy.

I nod, squaring my shoulders. "Ready as I'll ever be."

We pile into the car, a tangle of elbows and emotions. As Mama turns the key, I take one last look at the house that built me, the town that raised me.

The road stretches before us, a ribbon of promise, of possibility. And with each mile marker, I feel you near. Your love, your lessons, a compass pointing true north.

I finger the dog tag, its edges already familiar, already dear. "Faith. Family. Love," I whisper, a mantra and a vow.

I carry you with me, Daddy. Your strength, your wisdom, your unwavering belief. The seeds you planted, now blossoming in the light of a new day.

I don't know what this next chapter holds. But I know I'll face it with the courage you instilled, the faith you fostered. And when the road gets rough, when the storms roll in, I'll rub this tag and remember.

I am a oak, rooted deep. I am a Johnson, born to rise. And I am your daughter, forever and always.

Watch over me, Daddy. Guide my steps.

Your little girl, ready to fly,

Remi

CHAPTER FOUR

Dear Daddy,

I'm writing this from my dorm room, perched on the edge of a twin bed that feels both foreign and familiar. The air smells of fresh paint and possibility, the walls bare canvases waiting to be filled.

It's been a whirlwind, these first few weeks. A blur of orientation sessions and awkward introductions, of syllabi and social mixers. I feel like Alice, tumbled down the rabbit hole into a world both wondrous and strange.

I wish you could see it, Daddy. The way the sun dapples the quad, filtering through leaves just beginning to hint at autumn's approach. The hum of knowledge, of discovery, that seems to vibrate in every brick and beam.

But more than that, I wish you were here to steady me. To be my touchstone in a sea of newness, of uncertainty.

I knew it would be different, being away from home. From the rhythm and routine of the life I've always known. But I didn't expect to feel so untethered, so unmoored.

It's the little things that catch me off guard. The way my hand reaches for the phone, eager to share some small triumph or frustration, only to remember that you're not on the other end of the line. The way I scan the crowd at football games, half-expecting to see your face beaming back at me.

And it's the bigger things, too. The way my classmates talk about their dads, about summer fishing trips and father-daughter dances. The way they take for granted the luxury of a phone call, a bear hug, a shared slice of pie.

I don't resent them, Daddy. I don't begrudge their blessing. But sometimes, in the shadow of their ease, I feel the ache of your absence like a physical thing. A hollow in my chest, a catch in my throat.

Mama reminds me that I'm not alone. That I have a Father who sees, who knows, who holds me in the palm of His hand. And I cling to that truth, Daddy.

I cling to the faith you fostered, the assurance you instilled.

But there are moments, in the stillness of the night or the chaos of the day, when doubt creeps in like a thief. When I wonder if I have what it takes, if I'm strong enough, brave enough, to navigate this new world without your hand to guide me.

It's in those moments that I reach for your dog tag, the metal warm against my skin. A reminder of the man who taught me to stand tall, to trust in the unseen. The man who loved me beyond measure, beyond reason.

I hear your voice, a whisper in my heart. "You've got this, baby girl," you say, your eyes crinkled with certainty. "You were made for this, for such a time as this."

So I take a deep breath, Daddy. I square my shoulders and tip my chin toward the sky. I let your courage course through me, a river of resilience, of resolve.

I may stumble, may falter. I may have days when the ache of missing you feels like more than I can bear. But I will not crumble, will not fold.

I am your daughter, a Johnson through and through. And Johnsons? We rise.

Watch over me, Daddy. Steady my steps. And know that every day, in ways big and small, I carry you with me. My north star, my guiding light.

I love you. I miss you. And I'll make you proud.

Your little girl, all grown up,
Remi

***

Dear Daddy,

I'm sitting in the back of the lecture hall, my pen poised over a fresh page in my notebook. But the professor's words wash over me, a distant tide. My mind is a thousand miles away, lost in a sea of questions without answers.

It's my Intro to Philosophy class, a requirement for my major. I thought I was ready, eager even, to dive into the big questions. To grapple with the nature of existence, of morality, of truth.

But now, faced with the vastness of it all, I feel small. Unsteady. Like a sailor without a compass, a map with no legend.

We started with the classics, with Plato and Aristotle. Their words, dense and ancient, seemed to echo through the ages. A call to examine, to interrogate, the very foundations of our beliefs.

And I tried, Daddy. I tried to engage, to wrestle with the ideas like Jacob wrestling the angel. But the more I grappled, the more I felt the ground shift beneath my feet.

For the first time in my life, I'm confronting the notion that the truths I've always held dear, the faith that's been my bedrock, might not be as solid as I thought. That there are other ways of seeing the world, other lenses through which to view reality.

It's exhilarating, in a way. Like standing on the edge of a cliff, feeling the wind whip through your hair, the vast expanse of possibility stretching before you.

But it's terrifying, too. Because what if, in the pursuit of knowledge, of understanding, I lose sight of what's always anchored me? What if, in the whirlwind of new ideas and competing philosophies, I lose hold of the truth that's been my north star?

I think of the verses we used to recite together, huddled over my Bible. "Trust in the Lord with all your heart," you'd say, your voice a rumble of assurance. "And lean not on your own understanding."

But what does that mean, Daddy, in the face of so many divergent paths, so many different conceptions of the divine? How do I hold fast to my faith while still honoring the pursuit of truth, of wisdom?

I wish I could talk to you about this. Wish I could hear your perspective, your guidance. You always had a way of cutting through the noise, of finding the signal in the static.

I can picture you now, your brow furrowed in thought. "Remi, baby," you'd say, "faith isn't about having all the answers. It's about trusting the One who does. About walking in the light you've been given, even when the path isn't clear."

You'd remind me that it's okay to question, to wrestle. That God is big enough to handle my doubts, my uncertainties. That the pursuit of truth, when approached with humility and reverence, is an act of worship.

So I'm trying, Daddy. I'm trying to lean into the discomfort, the ambiguity. To trust that the same God who brought me this far will lead me onward, will light my path.

I'm learning to hold my faith with open hands. To let it breathe, to let it grow. To trust that the foundation you helped lay will weather the storms, will anchor me still.

And on the days when the doubts loom large, when the questions feel like more than I can bear, I'll remember your wisdom. Your steadfastness.

I'll remember that I am held, that I am known. That the God you taught me to trust is faithful, is true.

Watch over me, Daddy. Guide my steps. And know that in every question, every doubt, every flicker of faith, I carry you with me.

Your little seeker,

Remi

***

Dear Daddy,

It happened. The thing I've been dreading, the pain I've been bracing for since the moment I first stepped foot on this campus. Heartbreak.

His name was Jeremiah. A junior, a political science major with dreams of changing the world. He had a smile like sunshine and a mind like a steel trap, and when he looked at me, I felt seen. Heard. Understood.

We met at a rally, a protest against police brutality. I was holding a sign, my hands shaking with anger and grief. He was leading a chant, his voice a clarion call for justice.

In the midst of the chaos, our eyes met. A spark, a recognition. A sense that we were fighting the same battle, walking the same path.

We started talking, started dreaming. Late nights in the library, early mornings on the quad. He told me about his plans for law school, for a life spent advocating for the marginalized and oppressed. I told him about my love for art, for the power of stories to heal and transform.

For a moment, Daddy, I thought I'd found my person. My partner in this beautiful, broken world.

But then, as quickly as it began, it ended. A misunderstanding, a miscommunication. A realization that maybe we weren't on the same page after all.

I won't bore you with the details, with the he-said-she-saids. But suffice it to say, it hurt. It hurt like a physical ache, a hollow in my chest where hope used to be.

I wanted to call you, Daddy. Wanted to hear your voice, your wisdom. Wanted you to wrap me in your arms and tell me that it would be okay, that this too shall pass.

But you weren't there. Aren't here. And in the wake of that absence, I felt untethered. Unmoored.

I cried, Daddy. Cried until my eyes were swollen and my throat was raw. Cried for Jeremiah, for the future I thought we'd build. But mostly, I cried for you. For the fact that in my moment of deepest need, I couldn't turn to the one person who'd always been my rock, my refuge.

Mama did her best, over crackling phone lines and care packages full of cookies. She reminded me of my worth, of my strength. Reminded me that no man defines me, that my identity is rooted in something far deeper, far truer.

And she was right, of course. I know that, in my bones and in my blood. But still, the ache persisted. The sense of loss, of longing.

It was in that space, that liminal land between hurt and healing, that I found myself turning to my art. To the blank canvas and the open page, the only place where I could pour out my heart without fear of judgment or rejection.

I painted, Daddy. Painted through the tears and the turmoil, the anger and the ache. I painted sunrises and storms, deserts and oceans. I painted the contours of my own heart, the topography of my own becoming.

And in the process, I found solace. Strength. A reminder that even in the midst of pain, there is power. There is purpose.

I remembered your words, your lessons. The way you taught me to alchemize hurt into beauty, to find the gold in the grey. The way you showed me that true love, the kind that lasts, starts with loving myself.

So I'm picking up the pieces, Daddy. I'm mending my heart, one brushstroke at a time. I'm learning to trust the journey, to lean into the growth.

And I know, with a certainty that runs soul-deep, that you're with me. That your love, your legacy, is the canvas upon which I'll continue to paint my story.

Your little artist,

Remi

✳✳✳

Dear Daddy,

The sun is setting over the Potomac, painting the sky in shades of orange and gold. I'm sitting on the steps of the Lincoln Memorial, my sketchbook balanced on my knees. The marble is cool against my skin, a welcome respite from the humid heat of the day.

I come here often, when the weight of the world feels like too much to bear. When the pressures of school and relationships and the great big unknown threaten to overwhelm me. There's something about this place, about the grandeur and the gravity of it, that puts things in perspective. That reminds me of the bigger picture, the greater purpose.

Today, I needed that reminder more than ever. Needed a touchstone, a north star, to guide me back to myself.

It's been a week since Jeremiah and I parted ways, a week since my heart shattered like a dropped plate on a tile floor. A week of putting on a brave face, of going through the motions, while inside I felt like I was drowning. Like I was lost at sea without a life raft, a lighthouse.

But today, as I sat in my studio, staring at a blank canvas, something shifted. A flicker of light in the darkness, a whisper of hope in the hollows of my heart.

I thought of you, Daddy. Of the way you always knew how to make me feel better, how to coax a smile from my trembling lips. I could almost hear your voice, your laughter, echoing through the years and the miles.

"Remi, my love," you'd say, your eyes crinkling at the corners. "Don't you know that you are a masterpiece?

That you are fearfully and wonderfully made, crafted in the very image of God?"

You'd pull me close, your strong arms a fortress, a shield. "No boy, no heartbreak, can change that. Can diminish your worth or dim your light. You are a daughter of the King, a princess in His sight."

The tears came then, hot and fast and cleansing. Tears of grief and gratitude, of sorrow and surrender. I cried for the little girl who'd lost her anchor, for the young woman learning to stand on her own two feet. I cried for the love I'd lost and the love I had yet to find, in myself and in others.

And as I cried, I felt something loosen in my chest. A knot of pain and fear and self-doubt, unfurling in the light of your love, your legacy.

I picked up my brush, my hands shaking but sure. And I began to paint. Bold strokes, bright colors. A portrait of a girl becoming, a woman rising. A masterpiece in the making, flaws and all.

With each brushstroke, I felt a piece of myself return. A piece of the joy and the fire and the faith that's always been my birthright, my inheritance. I felt the truth of your words, your wisdom, etching itself onto my heart.

I am a masterpiece, Daddy. A work of art, a wonder to behold. Not because of what I do or who I'm with, but because of who I am. Because of Whose I am.

And that truth, that unshakeable, unassailable truth, is the bedrock upon which I'll build my life. The canvas upon which I'll paint my dreams, my destiny.

I miss you, Daddy. With every fiber of my being, I miss you. But I know that you're with me, that you're watching over me. That you're cheering me on from heaven's front row.

So I'll keep painting, keep becoming. Keep rising, one brushstroke at a time. And I'll do it all for you, for the love that never dies.

Your little masterpiece,

Remi

CHAPTER FIVE

Dear Daddy,

I'm sitting in my advisor's office, a sheaf of papers clutched in my trembling hands. Course catalogs, major requirements, internship applications. The detritus of a decision I've been dancing around for months, a future I've been afraid to face.

But I can't put it off any longer. Can't keep pretending that I have all the time in the world to figure out who I am, what I want. The clock is ticking, the deadlines looming. And I'm paralyzed, caught between the tug of my dreams and the weight of my fears.

I wish you were here, Daddy. Wish I could sit across from you at the kitchen table, a mug of your famous hot chocolate warming my hands. Wish I could pour out my heart, my hopes, and know that you'd understand. That you'd have the words, the wisdom, to guide me through this wilderness.

I've always known I wanted to make a difference, to leave my mark on the world. But the shape of that mark, the form of that difference, has always felt just out of reach. Like a word on the tip of my tongue, a melody I can't quite place.

I love my art, Daddy. Love the way it makes me feel, the way it allows me to express the inexpressible. But is it enough? Is it the path I'm meant to walk, the legacy I'm meant to leave?

I think of the issues that set my soul on fire. The injustices that keep me up at night, the wrongs I long to right. Racism, poverty, inequality. The systemic sins that stain our society, that tarnish the promise of our shared humanity.

I think of the activists and the advocates, the policy-makers and the change-makers. The ones who roll up their sleeves and get into the trenches, who fight the good fight even when the odds are stacked against them. And I wonder, is that where I'm called to be? Is that the arena where I'm meant to make my stand?

But then I think of you, Daddy. Of the way you poured yourself into your art, your craft. The way you found beauty in the broken places, hope in the hard times.

The way you used your gift to heal and to uplift, to shine a light in the darkness.

And I wonder, is that not also a form of activism? Is that not also a way to change the world, one heart at a time?

I'm torn, Daddy. Torn between the path of the artist and the path of the advocate. Between the studio and the streets, the canvas and the capitol.

I know I don't have to choose. Know that I can be both, that I can weave my passions together into a tapestry of purpose. But I'm scared, Daddy. Scared of making the wrong choice, of letting you down.

I close my eyes, breathe deep. And in the stillness, I feel you near. Feel your hand on my shoulder, your voice in my ear.

"Remi, my love," you whisper. "Don't you know that your very existence is an act of resistance? That your joy, your creativity, your fierce and tender heart, are a rebellion against a world that would try to dim your light?"

The tears come then, hot and cleansing. Tears of relief, of release. Tears of gratitude for a father who always saw me, who always believed in the bigness of my dreams.

I'm still not sure what the future holds, Daddy. Still not sure which path I'll choose. But I know that wherever I go, whatever I do, I'll carry you with me. Your love, your wisdom, your unwavering faith in the power of art to change the world.

I am my father's daughter, a force to be reckoned with. And I'm ready, Daddy. Ready to take on the world, one brushstroke at a time.

Your little activist,

Remi

****

Dear Daddy,

The decision is made, the forms are signed. As of today, I am officially a double major in Studio Art and African American Studies. A creator and a crusader, a dreamer and a doer.

I won't pretend it was easy, won't pretend I didn't second-guess myself a hundred times along the way. There were moments when I wondered if I was trying to do too much, be too much. Moments when the whispers of doubt and the specter of failure loomed large in my mind.

But every time I faltered, every time I felt my resolve start to crumble, I thought of you. Of the lessons you taught me, the legacy you left me.

I thought of those long summer nights in your workshop, the air thick with the scent of sawdust and varnish. The way you'd lean over your latest project, your brow furrowed in concentration, your hands steady and sure.

"Remi, baby," you'd say, your eyes meeting mine over the cluttered workbench. "Don't you ever let anyone tell you that your dreams are too big, your vision too grand. You were put on this earth to create, to imagine, to make manifest the beauty that lives inside you."

You'd hold up your latest creation, a gleam of pride in your eye. "This here, this is more than just a piece of wood or a hunk of metal. This is a piece of my soul, a testament to the power of the human spirit. When I make something, when I pour my heart into my craft, I'm not just making art. I'm making a statement, a declaration of my right to exist, to take up space, to leave my mark on the world."

Those words, Daddy, they branded themselves on my heart. Etched themselves into my bones. They became the compass by which I navigated the uncharted waters of my own becoming, the North Star by which I plotted my course.

And so, when the doubts come, when the fears rise up like floodwaters, I anchor myself in your wisdom. I remind myself that my art, my activism, are not separate streams but a single mighty river, flowing from the wellspring of your love, your legacy.

I am not choosing between my passions, but rather weaving them together into a tapestry of purpose. I am not diminishing my light, but rather casting it wider, brighter, illuminating the dark corners of injustice and inequality.

I think of the projects I'll undertake, the causes I'll champion. The way I'll use my art to amplify the voices of the silenced, to shine a light on the stories that have been erased or ignored. The way I'll use my studies to contextualize my creations, to ground them in the rich soil of our history, our heritage.

I think of the world I want to build, the legacy I want to leave. A world where every child has the chance to dream big, to color outside the lines. A world where black joy, black genius, black creativity are celebrated and uplifted. A world where the beauty of our diversity is not a threat but a promise, a testament to the boundless potential of the human spirit.

That's the world you dreamed of, Daddy. The world you worked for, the world you believed in with every fiber of your being. And that's the world I'll continue to fight for, to create, with every brushstroke, every essay, every act of defiant, joyful resistance.

I am my father's daughter, a force to be reckoned with. And I'm just getting started, Daddy. Just getting started.

Your little world-changer,

Remi

***

Dear Daddy,

Today, I walked across the stage at Georgetown, a diploma in my hand and a fire in my heart. As I moved the tassel from right to left, I swear I could feel you there beside me, your pride a palpable thing, your love a warm wind at my back.

We did it, Daddy. We made it to the mountaintop, just like you always said we would. Through the long nights and the early mornings, the tears and the triumphs, the setbacks and the breakthroughs. We climbed, step by step, hand in hand, until we reached the summit.

And what a view it is, Daddy. What a breathtaking, heart-stopping vista of possibility and promise. From up here, I can see the road ahead, winding and uncertain but brimming with potential. I can see the world I want to create, the change I want to make, shimmering on the horizon like a mirage made real.

But even as I revel in this moment, even as I savor the sweetness of this accomplishment, I can't help but feel a pang of bittersweetness, a shadow of sorrow amidst the celebrations.

Because you should be here, Daddy. You should be the one whooping and hollering from the stands, the one sweeping me up in a bone-crushing hug, the one beaming with pride as we pose for pictures, cap and gown and unbridled joy.

But life, in all its beautiful, brutal mystery, had other plans. And so I carry you with me, instead. In my heart, in my mind, in the very marrow of my bones. I carry your wisdom, your warmth, your unwavering belief in the power of education to transform lives, to shatter ceilings and break chains.

I think back to all the conversations we had, all the dreams we spun in the golden hours between dinner and bedtime. You'd sit me on your knee, your eyes sparkling with mischief and hope, and you'd ask me, "Remi, baby girl, what do you want to be when you grow up?"

And I'd rattle off a litany of possibilities, each one more outlandish than the last. An astronaut, a ballerina, a wizard, a queen. And you'd listen, your face a study in mock seriousness, before breaking into a grin and saying, "Well, why not? You can be anything you set your mind to, long as you're willing to work for it."

That faith, that unswerving conviction in my potential, was the greatest gift you ever gave me, Daddy. Greater than any toy or trinket, any material possession or earthly reward. You gave me the gift of belief, of confidence, of a deep and abiding sense of my own worth and my own power.

And it's that gift that I carried with me as I walked across that stage today, as I took my place among the ranks of the educated, the empowered, the unabashedly ambitious. It's that gift that I'll carry with me as I step out into the world, as I set out to make my mark, to leave this place better than I found it.

Because that's what you taught me, Daddy. That's the legacy you left me. A legacy of love, of learning, of a life lived in service to something greater than myself. A legacy of leadership, of trailblazing, of daring to dream big and fight hard and never, ever settle for less than I deserve.

I am my father's daughter, a graduate, a go-getter, a force to be reckoned with. And I'm just getting started, Daddy. Just getting started.

Your little scholar,

Remi

***

Dear Daddy,

It's been a month since I crossed that stage, a month since I stepped out into the world, newly minted degree in hand and dreams in heart. And what a month it's been, Daddy. What a whirlwind of job applications and interviews, of networking events and informational coffee dates.

But amidst the hustle and bustle, the excitement and the exhaustion, I've found myself facing a harsh reality, a sobering truth that no one prepared me for in the hallowed halls of academia.

The world, it seems, isn't quite ready for a firebrand like me. Isn't quite sure what to do with a young, black woman with a head full of ideas and a heart full of passion. The job market, for all its talk of diversity and inclusion, still favors the familiar, the safe, the neatly packaged and easily digestible.

I can't tell you how many times I've walked into an interview, head held high and resume polished to a shine, only to be met with barely concealed skepticism, with the unspoken question of "Are you sure you're in the right place?"

I've lost count of the polite rejections, the canned emails thanking me for my interest but informing me that they've decided to go with a candidate whose qualifications more closely align with their needs. And I can't help but wonder, Daddy, if those qualifications have more to do with the color of my skin than the content of my character.

It's enough to make a girl want to give up, to throw in the towel and settle for something less than her dreams. But then I remember you, Daddy. I remember the way you faced down adversity with a steady gaze and an unwavering spirit, the way you refused to let the world tell you who you could be or what you could achieve.

I remember the stories you told me, the tales of your own struggles and triumphs in a world that wasn't always kind to men like you. The way you had to fight tooth and nail for every opportunity, every chance to prove yourself, to show the world the brilliance and the beauty that lived inside you.

And I remember the way you never, ever gave up. The way you kept pushing, kept striving, kept believing in yourself and your worth, even when the world tried to tell you otherwise. The way you taught me to do the same, to hold my head high and my heart open, to never let anyone dim my light or steal my joy.

So I'm taking a page from your book, Daddy. I'm digging deep, tapping into that wellspring of resilience and determination that you planted in me all those years ago. I'm reminding myself that I am my ancestors' wildest dreams, that I am the culmination of generations of struggle and sacrifice, of hope and hard work.

I'm reminding myself that I am not alone in this fight, that I stand on the shoulders of giants, of trailblazers and change-makers who paved the way for me to be here, to have the opportunities and the options that they could only imagine.

And I'm reminding myself that this is just the beginning, that the road ahead may be rocky and the journey may be long, but the destination is worth it. Because the world needs my voice, Daddy. Needs my vision, my creativity, my fierce and tender heart.

I am my father's daughter, a force to be reckoned with. And I won't stop until I make you proud, until I build the life and the legacy that you always knew I could.

Your little world-shaker,

Remi

CHAPTER SIX

Dear Daddy,

I met someone. And before you start worrying, before you start sharpening your shotgun and practicing your stern father face, let me just say this: he's different, Daddy. He's special.

His name is Amare, and he's everything I never knew I needed. He's kind and smart and funny, with a heart as big as the sky and a smile that lights up the room. He's a man of faith, just like you, with a deep and abiding love for God and a commitment to living out his values in everything he does.

We met at church, of all places. I was running late, as usual, slipping into the back pew just as the first notes of the opening hymn began to swell. And there he was, sitting a few rows ahead of me, his head bowed in prayer and his shoulders broad and strong.

I don't know what it was, Daddy, but something about him just called to me. Maybe it was the way he sang, his voice rich and soulful, lifting up to the heavens like a prayer. Maybe it was the way he listened to the sermon, his brow furrowed in concentration, his Bible open and well-worn on his lap.

Or maybe, just maybe, it was the way he looked at me when we were introduced after the service, his eyes warm and curious, his hand firm and gentle in mine. Maybe it was the way he made me feel seen, really seen, for the first time in a long time.

We started talking, Amare and I. About our faith, our families, our hopes and dreams for the future. And with every conversation, every shared laugh and knowing glance, I could feel something growing between us, something tender and true.

He tells me about his work as a teacher, about his passion for mentoring young boys and helping them find their way in a world that isn't always kind to men like them. He tells me about his own struggles, his own moments of doubt and darkness, and how his faith has been his anchor, his guiding light.

And I tell him about you, Daddy. About the man you were, the love you gave, the legacy you left. I tell him about the hole in my heart, the ache that never quite goes away, and how I'm learning to live with it, to grow around it, like a tree around a stone.

He listens, Amare does. Really listens, with his whole heart and his whole being. And when I'm finished, when I've poured out my soul and laid bare my scars, he takes my hand in his and he prays. He prays for healing, for comfort, for the peace that surpasses all understanding.

And in that moment, Daddy, I feel something shift inside me. Something small and subtle, like a key turning in a lock. I feel a flicker of hope, a glimmer of possibility, like the first ray of sun after a long, dark night.

I don't know where this thing with Amare will go, Daddy. I don't know if he's the one, the man I'll spend my life with, the father of my children. But I do know this: he makes me happy, Daddy. He makes me feel safe and cherished and seen. And for right now, for this moment in time, that's enough.

I wish you were here to meet him, Daddy. To size him up and give him the third degree, to make sure he's good enough for your little girl. But I know that, somehow, you already know. That you're watching over me, smiling down from heaven, giving me your blessing.

Your little girl, all grown up,

Remi

***

Dear Daddy,

Tonight, Amare and I had a talk. A deep, soul-baring, heart-on-the-table kind of talk. The kind of talk that leaves you feeling raw and exposed, but also strangely light, like a burden has been lifted from your shoulders.

We were sitting on his couch, a bowl of popcorn between us and a movie playing softly in the background. And out of nowhere, he turned to me and said, "Remi, tell me about your dad."

It caught me off guard, Daddy. Caught me right in the throat, like a sudden lump of emotion. Because even after all this time, even after all the healing and the growing and the moving forward, talking about you isn't easy. It's like poking at a bruise, like prodding at a wound that's long since scarred over but still aches when the weather changes.

But something about the way Amare asked, something about the gentleness in his eyes and the care in his voice, made me want to open up. Made me want to let him in, to share with him the parts of myself that I usually keep hidden away.

So I did, Daddy. I told him everything. About the way you loved, fiercely and fully, with your whole heart on your sleeve. About the way you laughed, big and booming, like a clap of thunder on a summer day. About the way you danced, off-beat and unashamed, like the whole world was your stage.

I told him about your struggles, too. About the way the bottle sometimes called to you, like a siren song in the night. About the way you fought it, tooth and nail, day by day, step by step. About the way you never let it define you, never let it steal your joy or dim your light.

And I told him about the hole you left behind, the space in my life that nothing and no one can ever quite fill. About the way I miss you, every day, like a physical ache in my chest. About the way I still sometimes catch myself reaching for the phone, wanting to call you and tell you about my day, before remembering that you're not there to answer.

Amare listened, Daddy. He held me as I cried, as I poured out my heart and let the tears fall like rain. And when I was finished, when I was spent and empty and raw, he looked me in the eye and he said, "Remi, your dad was a hero. A real-life, honest-to-God hero. And

I know that, wherever he is, he's so proud of you. So proud of the woman you've become."

It was like a balm, Daddy. Like a cool cloth on a fevered brow. Because all my life, all I've ever wanted was to make you proud. To live up to the legacy you left, to be the kind of person you always knew I could be.

And hearing Amare say those words, hearing him affirm what I've always hoped in my heart to be true, was like a weight being lifted from my shoulders. Like a knot being untied in my chest.

I know we've still got a long way to go, Amare and I. I know that love isn't always easy, that it takes work and patience and a whole lot of grace. But I also know that, with him by my side, I feel stronger. More whole. More ready to face whatever the future holds.

And I know that, somewhere up there, you're smiling down on us. That you're giving us your blessing, your love, your endless supply of dad jokes.

I love you, Daddy. I miss you. And I'm doing my best to make you proud.

Your little girl, always,

Remi

***

Dear Daddy,

It's been a year since Amare and I first started dating, a year filled with laughter and love, with deep conversations and silly dance parties in the kitchen. And with each passing day, each shared moment and inside joke, I can feel myself falling deeper, can feel my heart opening up in ways I never thought possible.

But as much as I love him, Daddy, as much as I can see a future with him stretching out before me like a road map to forever, I'd be lying if I said I wasn't scared. Scared of taking that next step, of making that leap of faith into the great unknown.

Because marriage, Daddy... it's a big deal. It's a promise, a commitment, a sacred vow before God and man. And after watching you and Mama, after seeing the way you loved each other through thick and thin, through sickness and health, I know that it's not something to be entered into lightly.

I've been praying about it, Daddy. Every night, before I close my eyes, I've been asking God for guidance, for wisdom, for a sign that Amare is the one He's chosen for me. And every morning, when I wake up, I've been hoping to feel that sense of peace, that unshakeable certainty that this is the path I'm meant to walk.

But the truth is, Daddy, I'm not sure if I'll ever feel 100% ready. I'm not sure if anyone ever does. Because love, real love, the kind of love that lasts a lifetime... it's a risk. It's a leap of faith, a jump into the void with no guarantee of a soft landing.

And that's where you come in, Daddy. That's where I need your guidance, your wisdom, your gentle nudge in the right direction. I know you're not here to give me away at my wedding, to dance with me at the reception and embarrass me with your corny toasts. But I also know that you're never far, that you're always watching over me, cheering me on from the great beyond.

So I'm asking you, Daddy... what do you think? Is Amare the one for me? Is he the man you always hoped I'd find, the partner who will stand by my side through all of life's ups and downs? Is he worthy of your little girl's heart?

I close my eyes and I try to picture your face, try to imagine what you'd say if you were here beside me. And in my mind's eye, I see you smiling, see your eyes crinkling at the corners the way they always did when you were about to impart some fatherly wisdom.

"Remi, baby girl," I hear you say, your voice as warm and rich as honey. "Love isn't about finding the perfect person. It's about finding the person who makes you want to be your best self, who brings out the light inside you and helps you shine. It's about finding the person who feels like home, no matter where you are or what life throws your way."

"And from what I've seen," you continue, your hand reaching out to squeeze mine, "Amare is that person for you. He loves you, baby girl, with a love that's pure and true and strong. And he makes you happy, happier than I've ever seen you. So if you're asking for my blessing, if you're asking for my permission to take that leap... you've got it, sweetheart. You've got it in spades."

I feel a tear slip down my cheek, feel a wave of gratitude and love wash over me like a warm summer rain. Because even though you're not here, Daddy, even though I can't hold your hand or hug you tight... I can still feel you with me. I can still hear your voice in my heart, still feel your love guiding me forward.

And with that love, with that blessing... I think I'm ready, Daddy. Ready to take that leap, to say "yes" to forever with the man who feels like home.

Your little girl, all grown up,

Remi

Dear Daddy,

Last night, Amare got down on one knee. In the middle of the restaurant where we had our first date, with a ring that sparkled like a promise and a smile that could light up the darkest night, he asked me to be his wife. And with tears in my eyes and a heart so full it felt like it might burst, I said yes.

Yes to a lifetime of love and laughter, of joy and adventure. Yes to early morning coffees and late night slow dances in the living room. Yes to building a life together, brick by brick, hand in hand.

But even in the midst of my joy, Daddy, even in the giddy rush of excitement and love, I couldn't help but feel a pang of sadness. Because as much as I know that you're here with me in spirit, as much as I know that you're smiling down from heaven... I wish more than anything that you were here to share in this moment.

I wish you could have been there to give Amare your blessing in person, to shake his hand and look him in the eye and make sure he knows just how precious your little girl is. I wish you could have been there to hug me tight and tell me how proud you are, how happy you are to see me find a love like the one you and Mama shared.

Because your love story, Daddy... it's the stuff of legends. The way you two weathered every storm, the way you clung to each other even when the world was crumbling around you. The way you chose each other, day after day, even when it wasn't easy, even when it would have been simpler to walk away.

I think about your wedding photo, the one that used to hang in the hallway. You in your dapper suit, Mama in her lace gown, both of you beaming like you'd just won the lottery. And in a way, I guess you had. Because you found each other, two souls cut from the same cloth, two hearts beating in perfect sync.

I know your road wasn't always smooth, Daddy. I know there were times when your demons got the best of you, when the bottle called louder than your vows. But I also know that you never stopped fighting, never stopped trying to be the man Mama deserved. And in the end, your love was stronger than any addiction, any obstacle that life threw your way.

That's the kind of love I want, Daddy. That's the kind of love I pray for, the kind of love I've found in Amare. A love that can weather any storm, that can overcome any odds. A love that's built on faith and friendship, on respect and devotion.

I close my eyes and I picture our wedding day, picture myself walking down the aisle in a white dress, my heart so full it feels like it might take flight. And even though I know you won't be there to give me away, even though I know Mama will be the one to place my hand in Amare's... I know that you'll be with me, Daddy. I know that you'll be watching over us, your love a tangible presence, a blessing that will carry us through all the days of our lives.

So thank you, Daddy. Thank you for showing me what true love looks like, for setting the bar so high that I refused to settle for anything less.

I love you, Daddy. I miss you. And I can't wait to start this new chapter, to build a love that would make you proud.

Your little girl, forever and always,

Remi

CHAPTER SEVEN

Dear Daddy,

Today, I woke up a bride. I woke up to a room filled with sunlight and laughter, to Mama and my brides-maids buzzing around me like bees in a hive. I woke up to the smell of hairspray and perfume, to the rustle of taffeta and the clink of champagne glasses.

But even in the midst of the chaos, even in the whirlwind of preparation and excitement, I found myself stealing quiet moments. Moments to sit with you, to feel your presence, to imagine what this day would be like if you were here beside me.

I thought about our daddy-daughter dates, the ones we used to take every year on my birthday. The way you'd get all dressed up, your tie always a little crooked, your smile brighter than the candles on my cake. The way you'd take me to my favorite restaurant, the one with the pink lemonade and the endless breadsticks, and make me feel like the most special girl in the world.

I thought about the talks we had on those dates, the life lessons you'd impart between bites of spaghetti. The way you'd look me in the eye, your gaze so full of love and pride, and tell me that I could be anything, do anything, as long as I stayed true to myself and my faith.

And I thought about the dance we shared at my sweet sixteen, the way you twirled me around the room like a princess, your laughter mingling with mine. The way you held me close and whispered in my ear, "No matter how old you get, no matter where life takes you... you'll always be my little girl."

I'm holding those words close today, Daddy. I'm letting them wrap around me like a hug, like a benediction. Because as much as I wish you were here to walk me down the aisle, to give me away to the man of my dreams... I know that, in a way, you already have.

You gave me away every time you encouraged me to chase my dreams, every time you pushed me to be my best self. You gave me away every time you showed me what a good man looks like, what a loving husband and father should be.

And you're giving me away today, Daddy. With every step I take, with every vow I make... you're right there beside me, your hand in mine, your love a steady beat in my heart.

I wish you could see me, Daddy. I wish you could see the woman I've become, the life I've built. I wish you could see the way Amare looks at me, like I'm the answer to every prayer he's ever whispered. I wish you could see the way we fit together, two puzzle pieces finally finding their perfect match.

But even though you're not here in body, I know you're here in spirit. I know you're watching over me, your smile as bright as the sun. I know you're dancing with the angels, your laughter a joyful hymn in the heavens.

And I know that, when I stand at the altar and say "I do," when I pledge my heart and my life to the man who feels like home... you'll be right there with me, Daddy. Your love a blessing, your memory a treasure, your legacy a light that will guide me all the days of my life.

I love you, Daddy. I miss you. And I can't wait to start this new chapter, to build a love that would make you proud.

Your little girl, forever and always,

Remi

****

Dear Daddy,

I'm writing this from the honeymoon suite, my wedding dress draped over a chair and my heart so full it feels like it might burst. It's been a whirlwind of a day, a dream come true in every sense of the word. But amidst the joy and the celebration, the laughter and the tears, there was one moment that stood out. One moment that I know I'll carry with me for the rest of my life.

It was during the ceremony, right before Amare and I exchanged our vows. The pastor asked who gave this woman to be married to this man, and in that moment, Daddy, I swear I could feel you there beside me. I could feel your hand on my shoulder, your love wrapping around me like a warm embrace.

And as I stood there, my heart so full of emotion that I could barely speak, I made a silent vow of my own. A vow to honor your legacy, to live a life that would make you proud. A vow to love with the same fierce devotion, the same unwavering commitment that you showed to Mama and to us.

I know it won't always be easy, Daddy. I know that marriage is work, that it takes patience and forgiveness and a whole lot of grace. But I also know that I have the best role model in the world, the shining example of what true love looks like.

Because your love for Mama, Daddy... it was the stuff of legends. The way you cherished her, the way you treated her like a queen. The way you worked hard every day to provide for her, to build a life that would make her proud. The way you never let your struggles, your demons, dim the light of your love.

I remember the way you used to look at her, like she was the most beautiful woman in the world. The way you'd sneak kisses in the kitchen, the way you'd slow dance in the living room even when there was no music playing. The way you'd bring her flowers for no reason, just because you wanted to see her smile.

That's the kind of love I want to build with Amare, Daddy. A love that endures, that perseveres, that grows stronger with each passing year. A love that's rooted in friendship, in laughter, in the quiet moments that make up a life.

I know there will be challenges, Daddy. I know there will be days when the road feels steep and the burden feels heavy. But I also know that I have the strength to carry on, to keep climbing, to keep fighting for the love that you taught me to believe in.

And I know that, every step of the way, you'll be with me. Your love a compass, your wisdom a guide, your memory a blessing that I'll carry in my heart forever.

So thank you, Daddy. Thank you for showing me what it means to love with your whole heart, to give with your whole self. Thank you for setting the bar high, for challenging me to be the best version of myself. Thank you for being the kind of man, the kind of husband, that I can only hope to find in Amare.

I miss you, Daddy. I wish more than anything that you could be here to see the life I'm building, the love I'm cultivating. But I know that, in a way, you are. I know that your love lives on, in me and through me.

And I promise, Daddy. I promise to make you proud. To love with your strength, to live with your grace, to leave a legacy that would make you smile.

Your little girl, all grown up,

Remi

***

Dear Daddy,

Marriage is hard. I know that's not the most romantic thing to say, especially not when I'm still in the honeymoon phase, still basking in the glow of newlywed bliss. But it's the truth, Daddy. And it's a truth that I'm learning, day by day, hand in hand with the man I love.

It's the little things, the tiny annoyances that can fester into big resentments if you let them. It's the way Amare leaves his socks on the floor, the way he forgets to put the toilet seat down. It's the way I sometimes snap at him when I'm stressed, the way I retreat into myself when I'm feeling overwhelmed.

But it's also the big things, the fundamental differences in the way we see the world. It's the way Amare approaches problems head-on, while I like to take my time, to mull things over. It's the way he's a morning person, ready to tackle the day at the crack of dawn, while I'm a night owl who needs my beauty sleep.

There are days, Daddy, when I feel like throwing in the towel. When the dishes are piled high in the sink and the laundry is overflowing and we're both too stubborn to admit that we're wrong. There are moments when I wonder if we're cut out for this, if we have what it takes to go the distance.

But then I think of you and Mama, of the love that you built over a lifetime. I think of the way you weathered every storm, the way you clung to each other even when the world was falling apart. I think of the way you chose each other, day after day, even when it would have been easier to walk away.

And I remember, Daddy. I remember that love isn't a feeling, it's a choice. It's a decision to show up, to put in the work, to fight for the person you've pledged your life to. It's a commitment to grow together, to learn from each other, to become the best versions of yourselves.

So that's what I'm doing, Daddy. That's what Amare and I are doing, even when it's hard, even when it feels like an uphill battle. We're choosing each other, over and over again. We're learning to compromise, to communicate, to extend grace when we fall short.

We're learning that love is a verb, an action that requires effort and intention. That it's not just about the grand gestures, the fancy dinners and the lavish gifts. It's about the small, everyday acts of kindness, the little ways we show up for each other.

It's about the way Amare brings me coffee in bed, the way he rubs my feet after a long day. It's about the way I pack his lunch, the way I leave little love notes in his pockets. It's about the way we pray together, the way we lean on each other and on God.

And it's working, Daddy. Slowly but surely, we're building a love that will stand the test of time. A love that's rooted in friendship, in laughter, in the quiet moments that make up a life.

I know we have a long way to go, Daddy. I know there will be more challenges, more obstacles to overcome. But I also know that we have what it takes, that we have the strength and the faith and the commitment to see this through.

And I know that, every step of the way, you'll be with us. Your love a beacon, your wisdom a guide, your memory a blessing that we'll carry in our hearts forever.

Thank you, Daddy. For everything.

Your little girl, learning to love like you did,

Remi

Dear Daddy,

It's been a year since I said "I do," a year since I started this crazy, beautiful, messy journey called marriage. And what a year it's been, Daddy. What a rollercoaster of laughter and tears, of triumphs and challenges, of love in all its raw and imperfect glory.

There have been moments of pure joy, moments that took my breath away with their sweetness. The lazy Sunday mornings, tangled up in each other's arms, the rest of the world fading away. The impromptu dance parties in the kitchen, the inside jokes that never get old. The way Amare's face lights up when I walk in the room, the way my heart still skips a beat when he reaches for my hand.

But there have also been moments of struggle, moments when I've had to dig deep and fight for the love we've built. The arguments over silly things, the misunderstandings that spiral out of control. The times when we've both been too stubborn to bend, too proud to be the first to apologize. The nights when we've gone to bed angry, the hurt and the frustration hanging heavy in the air.

It's in those moments, Daddy, that I've had to lean on the lessons you taught me. The lessons about patience, about forgiveness, about choosing love even when it's hard. The lessons about putting God at the center, about trusting in His plan even when the path is unclear.

I remember one particularly tough patch, a few months into our marriage. Amare and I were both stretched thin, stressed out with work and bills and the everyday pressures of life. We were snapping at each other constantly, finding fault in every little thing.

It felt like we were drifting apart, like the spark that had brought us together was slowly fading away.

But then, one night, as we lay in bed with our backs turned to each other, I heard Amare's voice, soft and tender in the darkness. "I'm sorry," he whispered, reaching for my hand. "I know I haven't been the best husband lately. But I love you, Remi. I love you more than anything in this world. And I'm willing to do whatever it takes to make this work."

In that moment, Daddy, I felt a rush of love so strong it brought tears to my eyes. Because I knew, deep in my bones, that this man was my forever. That he was the one I wanted to build a life with, to weather every storm with, to grow old and gray with.

So we talked, Daddy. We stayed up all night, pouring out our hearts, sharing our fears and our dreams. We made a plan, a commitment to put each other first, to make our marriage a priority. We prayed together, asking God to guide us, to give us the strength and the wisdom to love each other well.

And slowly but surely, things got better. We learned to communicate, to compromise, to extend grace when we fell short. We learned to cherish the little moments, to find joy in the everyday. We learned to lean on each other, to be each other's safe place in a world that can be so harsh and unforgiving.

It hasn't been easy, Daddy. Marriage never is. But it's been worth it, every single step of the way. Because I know that, with Amare by my side, with God as our guide, there's nothing we can't face, nothing we can't overcome.

And I know that, somewhere up there, you're smiling down on us. That you're proud of the love we've built, the commitment we've made. That you're cheering us on, every step of the way.

I love you, Daddy. I miss you. And I promise to keep making you proud, to keep building a marriage that honors your legacy.

Your little girl, forever and always,

Remi

CHAPTER EIGHT

Dear Daddy,

I'm sitting here, staring at a little plastic stick with two pink lines. Two pink lines that have changed everything, that have tilted my world on its axis and sent my heart soaring into the stratosphere. Two pink lines that mean I'm going to be a mother, that a new life is growing inside me.

I'm pregnant, Daddy. Pregnant with your grandchild, with the next generation of our family tree. And I'm terrified and excited and overwhelmed all at once, a kaleidoscope of emotions swirling inside me like a whirlwind.

I found out this morning, in the quiet stillness of the bathroom. Amare was still sleeping, his soft snores drifting from the bedroom. I'd been feeling off for a few weeks, tired and queasy and out of sorts. But I chalked it up to stress, to the crazy pace of our lives. I never imagined... I never dreamed...

But then I remembered. Remembered the way my body felt different, the way my breasts were tender and my sense of smell was heightened. Remembered the way I'd burst into tears over a commercial, the way I'd been craving pickles and peanut butter at all hours of the day and night.

So I took the test, my hands shaking as I unwrapped the little foil package. And when I saw those two pink lines, when the realization hit me like a lightning bolt... oh, Daddy. I wish you could have been there. I wish I could have shared that moment with you, could have seen the joy and the wonder and the love in your eyes.

Because I know, deep in my bones, that you would have been the most amazing grandfather. That you would have doted on this child, would have spoiled them rotten with love and attention. That you would have been their fiercest protector, their most ardent champion, their safe harbor in a world that can be so stormy.

I can picture it now, Daddy. You, with a little one perched on your knee, your face alight with laughter. You, patiently teaching them how to bait a hook, how to throw a perfect spiral. You, wrapped around their little finger, unable to say no to their every whim and wish.

But even though you're not here, even though you won't get to hold this child in your arms... I know that you'll be with us, Daddy. I know that your love, your legacy, will live on through them. That they'll know you through the stories I'll tell, through the lessons I'll pass down, through the love that I'll pour into them with every breath.

I'm scared, Daddy. Scared of the responsibility, of the weight of this new role. Scared that I won't know what to do, that I'll make mistakes, that I'll fail in all the ways that matter. But I'm also excited, Daddy. Excited to meet this little person, to watch them grow and learn and become. Excited to experience the kind of love that I know you felt for me, the kind of love that moves mountains and parts seas.

And I'm grateful, Daddy. Grateful for the man that you were, for the father that you taught me to look for. Grateful for Amare, for the partner and the husband and the soon-to-be dad that he is. Grateful for this miracle, this blessing, this gift of new life.

I love you, Daddy. I miss you. And I promise to make you proud, to raise this child with the values and the faith and the love that you instilled in me.

Your little girl, about to be a mama,

Remi

P.S. - It's a boy, Daddy. We just found out. And his name... his name is going to be Joseph. After you. Because you were the best man I ever knew. And I want my son to grow up to be just like his grandpa.

***

Dear Daddy,

I'm scared. Scared in a way I've never been before, in a way that keeps me up at night, my mind racing and my heart pounding. I'm scared of failing, of falling short, of not being enough for this tiny life that's depending on me.

I thought I was ready, Daddy. I thought I had it all figured out. I read the books and took the classes, I decorated the nursery and packed the hospital bag. But now, as my due date draws closer, as the reality of motherhood looms large on the horizon... I feel like I'm drowning, like I'm in over my head and there's no lifeline in sight.

I worry about everything, Daddy. About the kind of world I'm bringing this child into, about the challenges and the heartaches they'll face. About the kind of mother I'll be, about the mistakes I'll make and the scars I'll leave. About the parts of myself I'll lose, the dreams I'll have to put on hold, the woman I'll have to become.

I wish you were here, Daddy. Wish I could crawl into your lap and bury my face in your chest, like I did when I was little and the world felt too big and too scary. Wish I could hear your voice, your wisdom, your reassurance that everything will be alright.

Because you always knew what to say, Daddy. You always knew how to soothe my fears and dry my tears, how to make me feel brave and strong and capable. You had a way of putting things into perspective, of reminding me of what really mattered, of pointing me back to the truth that never changes.

I can almost hear you now, your voice soft and steady in my ear. "Remi, baby girl," you'd say, "I know you're scared. I know you feel like you're not enough. But let me tell you something, sweetheart. You are exactly the mother this child needs. You are the only one who can love them the way they need to be loved, who can guide them the way they need to be guided, who can be there for them in all the ways that matter."

"And you won't be perfect, baby. You'll make mistakes and you'll have bad days, you'll lose your temper and you'll say things you regret. But that's okay, Remi. That's part of being human, part of being a parent. What matters is that you keep showing up, that you keep trying, that you keep loving with everything you've got."

"And when you feel like you can't do it, when you feel like you're failing and falling apart... that's when you lean on your faith, baby girl. That's when you turn to the One who made you, who knows you inside and out, who has a plan and a purpose for your life. That's when you trust that He will give you the strength and the wisdom and the grace to be the mother He's called you to be."

Oh, Daddy. I'm clinging to those words now, holding them close to my heart like a lifeline. Because I know you're right. I know that God has brought me to this moment, to this child, for a reason. I know that He will equip me and empower me, that He will be with me every step of the way.

And I know that, even though you're not here in body, you're here in spirit. That your love and your legacy will live on through me, through this child, through the generations to come. That you'll be watching over us, cheering us on, guiding us with your unseen hand.

I love you, Daddy. I miss you. And I promise to make you proud, to be the mother you always knew I could be.

Your little girl, learning to be brave,

Remi

***

Dear Daddy,

He's here. Your grandson, your namesake, the little boy who has stolen my heart and changed my world forever. Joseph Amare, born on a rainy Tuesday morning, his tiny face scrunched up and his little fists waving in the air.

Oh, Daddy. If you could see him. If you could hold him in your arms and breathe in his sweet, newborn scent. If you could feel the way he nestles into my chest, the way his tiny hand wraps around my finger like a promise. He's perfect, Daddy. Perfect in every way.

The moment they placed him on my chest, the moment I heard his first cry... it was like the world stopped spinning, like everything faded away and all that mattered was this tiny, precious life. I looked into his eyes, Daddy, and I saw a piece of you. I saw your strength and your kindness, your humor and your heart. I saw the legacy of love that you left behind, the seeds of faith that you planted in me.

And in that moment, Daddy, all my fears and doubts and worries just melted away. Because I knew, with a certainty that took my breath away, that I was made for this. That God had chosen me to be this child's mother, to guide him and nurture him and love him with everything I had.

It hasn't been easy, Daddy. The sleepless nights and the endless diapers, the sore nipples and the hormonal tears. There are moments when I feel like I'm drowning, when I wonder if I'm doing it right, if I'm giving him what he needs. But then he looks at me, Daddy. He looks at me with those big, trusting eyes, and he smiles that gummy, toothless smile... and I know that I'm exactly where I'm meant to be.

Amare has been amazing, Daddy. He's taken to fatherhood like a duck to water, like he was born to wear spit-up on his shirt and sing off-key lullabies. He changes diapers and gives baths, he rocks Joseph to sleep and tells him stories of the man he's named after. He looks at our son with a love so fierce and so pure that it takes my breath away, that it reminds me of the way you used to look at me.

I wish you were here, Daddy. Wish you could be a part of these precious, fleeting moments. Wish you could watch Joseph grow and learn and become, wish you could teach him how to ride a bike and throw a ball and be a good man. But I know that you're here in spirit, Daddy. I know that you're watching over us, that you're smiling down from heaven with pride and joy.

And I promise you, Daddy. I promise to tell Joseph all about you, to keep your memory alive in his heart. I promise to raise him with the values and the faith that you instilled in me, to teach him to love God and serve others and stand up for what's right. I promise to be the mother you always knew I could be, to give him roots and wings and everything in between.

Because that's what you did for me, Daddy. You loved me and guided me, you challenged me and believed in me. You showed me what it means to be a parent, to lay down your life for your child. And I will spend the rest of my days trying to live up to your example, trying to be the mother that Joseph deserves.

I love you, Daddy. I miss you. And I thank you, from the bottom of my heart, for the gift of your love and your legacy.

Your little girl, now a mama,

Remi

***

Dear Daddy,

Joseph is six months old today. Six months of sleepless nights and endless love, of first smiles and first rolls, of watching in awe as this tiny human grows and changes right before my eyes. Six months of being a mother, of learning and stumbling and finding my way.

And with each passing day, Daddy, I find myself thinking of you more and more. I find myself wondering what kind of grandfather you would have been, what kind of relationship you would have had with your grandson. I find myself longing to share these moments with you, to see the pride and the joy in your eyes.

Because I know, Daddy. I know that you would have been an amazing grandfather. I know that you would have doted on Joseph, that you would have spoiled him rotten with love and attention. I know that you would have been his biggest fan, his fiercest protector, his safe haven in a world that can be so uncertain.

I see so much of you in him already, Daddy. In the way he furrows his brow when he's concentrating, in the way he chuckles deep in his belly when he's amused. In the way he loves with his whole heart, in the way he lights up the room with his smile. He has your spirit, Daddy. Your zest for life, your unshakable faith, your boundless capacity for love.

And I promise you, Daddy. I promise to nurture that spirit, to fan those flames. I promise to raise Joseph with the values and the principles that you held so dear, to teach him to love God and serve others and fight for what's right. I promise to tell him about the man he's named after, to keep your memory alive in his heart and in our home.

Because that's the legacy you left, Daddy. A legacy of love and faith, of courage and compassion. A legacy that lives on in me, in Joseph, in the generations to come. A legacy that I will cherish and honor for the rest of my days.

There are moments, Daddy. Moments when the weight of this responsibility feels like too much to bear, when the fear of failing threatens to overwhelm me. Moments when I wonder if I'm strong enough, if I'm wise enough, if I'm enough, period.

But then I remember, Daddy. I remember the way you believed in me, the way you saw the best in me even when I couldn't see it myself. I remember the way you taught me to lean on God, to trust in His plan and His purpose, to find my strength in Him. And I know, Daddy. I know that I'm not alone in this journey, that I have a Father who will never leave me or forsake me.

And I have Joseph, Daddy. This beautiful, perfect, miraculous gift of a child. This living, breathing reminder of the love that created him, of the hope and the promise that he holds. When I look at him, Daddy, I see the future. I see the world as it could be, as it should be. And I feel a fierce, unshakable determination to make that world a reality, to give him the life and the legacy that he deserves.

So I will keep going, Daddy. I will keep learning and growing and becoming the mother that God has called me to be. I will keep loving with everything I have, keep pouring my heart and my soul into this precious child. And I will keep holding onto the faith that you taught me, the faith that sustains me and guides me and gives me hope.

I love you, Daddy. I miss you. And I thank you, for everything.

Your little girl, always,

Remi

CHAPTER NINE

Dear Daddy,

The years are flying by, slipping through my fingers like grains of sand. It seems like just yesterday I was rocking Joseph to sleep, breathing in his newborn scent and marveling at the miracle of his tiny, perfect form. And now, here he is, a little boy full of energy and curiosity, a little boy who looks more and more like you with each passing day.

Oh, Daddy. How I wish you could see him. How I wish you could hear the way he laughs, watch the way he runs and jumps and climbs with a fearless abandon. How I wish you could answer his endless questions, listen to his wild imaginings, be dazzled by the way his mind works.

He asks about you, Daddy. All the time. He wants to know what you were like, what made you laugh, what made you proud. He pores over the old photo albums, his little fingers tracing your face, his eyes wide with wonder and longing.

And I tell him, Daddy. I tell him everything. I tell him about the way you loved, the way you lived, the way you left an indelible mark on every life you touched. I tell him about the lessons you taught me, the values you instilled, the faith you passed down like a precious heirloom.

I tell him about the sacrifices you made, the battles you fought, the victories you won. I tell him about your time in the Navy, about the way you served with honor and courage, about the way you wore your uniform with a quiet, unshakable pride.

And he drinks it all in, Daddy. He hangs on every word, his little face rapt with attention. He asks to hear the stories again and again, never tiring of the tales of his grandpa, the hero he never got to meet.

But it's not just the stories, Daddy. It's the legacy, too. The legacy of service, of putting others before yourself, of standing up for what's right no matter the cost. That's the legacy I see in my brothers, in the way they've followed in your footsteps, in the way they've dedicated their lives to something greater than them-selves.

Michael, so strong and steady, a rock in the chaos of the world. Kwame, so quick and clever, a shining light in the darkness. And Kofi, my sweet baby brother, all grown up and blazing his own trail. All of them, Daddy. All of them carrying a piece of you, all of them living out the lessons you taught us.

And now, it's my turn. My turn to pass those lessons on, to share those stories, to keep your memory alive in the hearts of the next generation. It's a responsibility I don't take lightly, Daddy. A sacred trust, a precious gift.

Because I know, Daddy. I know that the way we remember you, the way we honor you, the way we live out your legacy... that's how we keep you with us. That's how we make sure that you're never really gone, that your light never truly goes out.

And so I will keep telling the stories, Daddy. I will keep passing down the lessons, keep living out the values. I will keep loving with everything I have, keep serving with everything I am. And I will keep watching in awe as your grandson grows and learns and becomes, as he takes his place in the tapestry of our family history.

Because that's the gift you gave us, Daddy. The gift of a life well-lived, a love well-loved, a legacy that will endure for generations to come.

I love you, Daddy. I miss you. And I promise to keep your memory alive, to keep your light shining bright.

Your little girl, always,

Remi

***

Dear Daddy,

Today, Joseph and I sat on the porch, a shoebox full of memories balanced on my lap. The sun was setting, painting the sky in shades of orange and pink, and the air was heavy with the scent of honeysuckle and nostalgia.

"Mama," Joseph said, his little voice filled with curiosity, "can you tell me more about Grandpa? About what he was like when you were a little girl?"

And so I did, Daddy. I opened the box and I opened my heart, letting the memories spill out like treasures, like gems glinting in the fading light.

I showed him the pictures, Daddy. The faded Polaroids and the glossy prints, the snapshots of a life well-lived. Pictures of you in your Navy uniform, young and strong and proud. Pictures of you and Mama on your wedding day, radiant with joy and love. Pictures of you holding me as a baby, your face alight with wonder and awe.

I told him the stories behind the pictures, Daddy. The funny ones that made us laugh until we cried, the poignant ones that brought tears to our eyes. I told him about the time you tried to teach me to ride a bike, about the way you bandaged my skinned knees and dried my tears. I told him about the Christmases and the birthdays, the family vacations and the Sunday dinners.

And then, Daddy, I told him about your service. About the sacrifices you made, the courage you showed, the duty you fulfilled. I told him about the long deployments, about the way you missed birthdays and holidays and first steps. I told him about the way you served with honor and integrity, about the way you put your life on the line for your country and your comrades.

Joseph listened, Daddy, his eyes wide with wonder and respect. He traced his little fingers over the medals and the ribbons, the tangible reminders of your bravery and your dedication. And I could see it in his face, Daddy. I could see the pride and the admiration, the seed of service taking root in his young heart.

"I want to be like Grandpa," he said, his voice filled with determination. "I want to be brave and strong and help people, just like he did."

Oh, Daddy. If you could have heard him. If you could have seen the way his face lit up, the way his little chest puffed out with purpose and conviction. It was like looking in a mirror, like seeing a reflection of you in his earnest eyes.

And I knew, in that moment, that your legacy would live on. That the values you lived by, the principles you fought for, the love you gave so freely... they would continue to shape and guide the generations to come.

Because that's who you were, Daddy. A hero, a role model, a shining example of what it means to live a life of service and sacrifice. And that's who Joseph will be, too. I can feel it in my bones, see it in the set of his jaw and the fire in his eyes.

He is your grandson, Daddy. Your flesh and blood, your living legacy. And I will spend the rest of my days making sure he knows it, making sure he understands the depth of the heritage he carries, the weight of the mantle he will one day bear.

Because that's the gift you gave us, Daddy. The gift of a life well-lived, a love well-loved, a legacy that will endure for generations to come.

I love you, Daddy. I miss you. And I promise to keep your memory alive, to keep your light shining bright.

Your little girl, always,

Remi

****

Dear Daddy,

Today was a day I'll never forget, a day that brought me right back to my childhood, to those golden afternoons spent walking to Grandma's house, my little hand safe in yours. Only this time, Daddy, I was the one leading the way, my own child's hand clutched tight in mine.

It was Joseph's idea, Daddy. He's been begging me for weeks to take him to see the house where you grew up, the place where so many of our family's memories were made. And so, on a sunny Saturday morning, we set off, just the two of us, on a pilgrimage of sorts.

As we walked, Daddy, I felt a rush of memories wash over me. The sound of your laughter, the warmth of your smile, the safety of your presence. I could almost hear your voice, could almost feel your hand guiding me, just like it did all those years ago.

And when we turned the corner, when that familiar little house came into view... oh, Daddy. The tears came before I could stop them, a flood of emotion that took my breath away. Because for a moment, just for a moment, it was like you were there with us, like no time had passed at all.

Joseph looked up at me, his little face filled with concern. "Mama, why are you crying?" he asked, his voice soft and tender.

"Because I'm happy, baby," I told him, wiping my eyes with the back of my hand. "Happy and sad and grateful, all at the same time. This place... it holds so many special memories for me, memories of your grandpa and the love he gave so freely."

And so we sat on the front steps, Daddy, just like you and I used to do. We ate the peanut butter sandwiches I'd packed, and I told Joseph the stories, the same stories you used to tell me. Stories of your boyhood adventures, of the mischief you and Uncle Isaac used to get into, of the love and the laughter that filled those walls.

Joseph listened, Daddy, his eyes wide with wonder and delight. He asked questions and made observations, his little mind working overtime to understand, to imagine, to connect. And I could see it happening,

Daddy. I could see the bond forming, the thread that ties him to you, to our family, to our history.

As we walked home, hand in hand, Joseph looked up at me with a smile that could light up the world. "Mama," he said, "I'm glad we went to Grandpa's house today. It made me feel close to him, even though I never got to meet him."

Oh, Daddy. The wisdom of children, the purity of their hearts. In that moment, I realized that this is how we keep you alive, how we honor your memory and your legacy. By sharing the stories, by passing down the love, by connecting the generations in a tapestry of remembrance and hope.

Because that's what you taught me, Daddy. That's the gift you gave me, the gift I now give to my son. The gift of roots and wings, of knowing where we come from and where we're going. The gift of a love that transcends time and space, a love that lives on in the hearts of those we leave behind.

I love you, Daddy. I miss you. And I promise to keep taking those walks, to keep telling those stories, to keep your memory alive in the heart of your grandson.

Your little girl, always,

Remi

***

Dear Daddy,

Today, I watched your legacy come to life before my very eyes. I watched as your grandson, your namesake, picked up a paintbrush and made his first strokes on a canvas, his little face scrunched up in concentration and joy. And oh, Daddy, it took my breath away.

You see, ever since Joseph was old enough to hold a crayon, he's been drawn to art. To color and shape and form, to the magic of creating something beautiful out of nothing at all. And as he's grown, as his skills have developed and his passion has deepened, I've seen more and more of you in him.

I've seen it in the way he loses himself in his art, in the way the world falls away and all that exists is the canvas and the colors and the feelings spilling out of his heart. I've seen it in the way he sees beauty in the ordinary, in the way he finds inspiration in the most unlikely of places.

And today, Daddy, I saw it in the way he picked up your old brushes, the ones I've kept all these years as a tangible reminder of your talent and your passion. I saw it in the way his eyes lit up, in the way his hands moved with a sureness and a grace that belied his young years.

We spent the whole afternoon in the studio, Daddy. Just Joseph and me, surrounded by your old easels and your half-finished canvases, your sketches and your paint-splattered aprons. And as I watched him work, as I watched the colors blooming beneath his brush like flowers in the spring, I felt a rush of emotions so deep and so powerful that it nearly brought me to my knees.

Pride, Daddy. Pride in the boy he is and the man he will become, pride in the gifts he's been given and the way he uses them to make the world a more beautiful place. Gratitude, for the legacy you've left us, for the love and the lessons and the laughter that still echo through our lives. And a bittersweet longing, Daddy, for the moments we'll never get to share, for the art you'll never get to make together.

But even in the midst of that longing, Daddy, there was joy. Joy in knowing that your spirit lives on, that your passion and your creativity have found new life in the hands and the heart of your grandson. Joy in seeing the threads that connect us, the way our stories intertwine and overlap and create a tapestry of love and memory and hope.

And as the sun began to set and the light turned golden through the studio windows, I put my arm around Joseph's shoulders and I told him the story. The story of his grandpa, the artist who could make magic with a brush and a bit of paint. The story of the man who taught me to see the world through eyes of wonder, who showed me the power of creating something beautiful and true.

Joseph listened, Daddy, his eyes shining with pride and awe. And when I was finished, when the last word had faded into the quiet of the studio, he turned to me with a smile that could light up the world.

"I want to be just like Grandpa," he said, his voice filled with determination and love. "I want to make art that makes people feel something, just like he did."

Oh, Daddy. In that moment, I saw the future stretching out before us, bright and beautiful and filled with possibility. And I knew, with a certainty that took my breath away, that your legacy would live on. That the gifts you gave us, the love you shared with us, would continue to grow and flourish and bear fruit for generations to come.

I love you, Daddy. I miss you. And I promise to keep nurturing the seeds you planted, to keep watering the garden of creativity and passion and joy that you left behind.

Your little girl, always,

Remi

CHAPTER TEN

Dear Daddy,

I'm writing this letter with shaking hands and a heart so full it feels like it might burst. I'm writing it from the front row of an auditorium, where in just a few moments, I'll watch our boy walk across the stage and receive his high school diploma. I'm writing it with tears in my eyes and a lump in my throat, because I can't believe that this day has come, that the tiny baby I once held in my arms is now a young man ready to take on the world.

Oh, Daddy. I wish you were here. I wish you could see him, could see the person he's become. I wish you could be sitting next to me, your arm around my shoulders, your eyes shining with pride. I wish we could share this moment, this milestone, this momentous occasion in the life of our family.

But even though you're not here in body, Daddy, I know you're here in spirit. I know you're watching over us, your love and your light shining down on us like the warmest of suns. I know that every step Kwame takes, every achievement he earns, every dream he chases, you're right there with him, cheering him on from the heavens.

And what a journey it's been, Daddy. What a ride, full of ups and downs and twists and turns. I think back to those early days, when Kwame was just a tiny bundle in my arms, so small and so perfect and so full of promise. I think back to the sleepless nights and the endless diaper changes, the first steps and the first words, the laughter and the tears and the love that grew deeper with every passing day.

I think about the challenges we've faced, the obstacles we've overcome. The times when I didn't know if I was doing it right, if I was being the mother he needed me to be. The times when I leaned on your memory, on your wisdom, on the lessons you taught me about love and strength and perseverance.

And I think about the joys we've shared, the triumphs we've celebrated. The art shows and the honor rolls, the basketball games and the prom nights. The quiet moments and the belly laughs, the heart-to-hearts and the bear hugs. The love that has sustained us, the love that has made us who we are.

And now, here we are, Daddy. Here we are on the cusp of a new chapter, a new adventure, a new beginning. Here we are, watching our boy spread his wings and take flight, ready to soar to heights we can only imagine.

I'm so proud of him, Daddy. I'm so proud of the man he's become, of the heart he has and the light he brings to the world. I'm so proud of the way he's grown, the way he's learned, the way he's loved. I'm so proud of the legacy he carries, the legacy of a grandfather he never met but whose spirit lives on in every breath he takes.

And I'm so grateful, Daddy. Grateful for the gift of this child, this miracle, this beating heart outside my own body. Grateful for the love that made him, the love that raised him, the love that will always be his guiding star. Grateful for the memories we've made, the moments we've shared, the laughter and the tears and the joy that have woven us together, stitch by stitch, into a tapestry of family and forever.

The music is starting now, Daddy. The procession is beginning, and I can see Kwame in the line, his cap and gown a brilliant blue, his smile brighter than the sun. And as I watch him take his first steps towards the future, towards the life that awaits him, I feel you beside me, your hand in mine, your heart beating in time with my own.

I love you, Daddy. I miss you. And I promise to keep making you proud, to keep living the legacy you left us, to keep loving with every fiber of my being.

Your little girl, always,

Remi

***

Dear Daddy,

The ceremony is over, the diplomas handed out, the caps tossed high into the air. And as I sit here in the quiet of my bedroom, the house still buzzing with the energy of celebration, I find myself reflecting on the journey that brought us here, on the road we've traveled and the love that has carried us through.

I think about the day Kwame was born, the moment they placed him in my arms and the world shifted on its axis. I think about the promise I made to you then, the vow I whispered to the heavens as I cradled our boy close to my heart. The promise to love him fiercely, to guide him gently, to give him roots and wings and everything in between.

And oh, Daddy, I've tried. I've tried to be the mother you always knew I could be, to pour every ounce of love and wisdom and strength into the shaping of his heart and his mind and his soul. I've tried to teach him the things that matter, the values and the virtues that will serve as his compass as he navigates the twists and turns of life.

I've taught him about faith, about the power of believing in something bigger than himself. I've taught him about compassion, about the importance of seeing the humanity in every person he meets. I've taught him about resilience, about the courage it takes to get back up when life knocks you down.

But more than anything, Daddy, I've taught him about love. About the kind of love that you modeled for us, the kind of love that is patient and kind and never fails. The kind of love that puts others first, that sacrifices and serves and gives without counting the cost. The kind of love that is the very heartbeat of our family, the pulse that echoes through the generations.

And as I've watched Kwame grow, as I've seen the seeds of that love take root and blossom in his heart, I've been in awe of the man he's becoming. The way he leads with grace and humility, the way he treats others with kindness and respect. The way he uses his gifts and his talents to make the world a little bit brighter, a little bit better than he found it.

I've seen your spirit in him, Daddy. Your quiet strength, your gentle wisdom, your unwavering faith.

I've seen the way he carries your legacy forward, the way he honors your memory with every breath he takes and every step he makes.

And I've seen the way he loves, Daddy. The way he loves with his whole heart, his whole being. The way he pours himself out in service to others, the way he goes out of his way to be a light in the darkness. The way he loves me, his mama, with a fierceness and a tenderness that takes my breath away.

I know that the road ahead won't always be easy for him, that there will be challenges and obstacles and moments when he feels like giving up. But I also know that he has everything he needs to face whatever lies ahead, that he has the tools and the wisdom and the love that will guide him through.

And he has you, Daddy. He has the legacy you left us, the example you set, the love you poured into us. He has the knowledge that no matter where he goes or what he does, he has a father in heaven who is always watching over him, always cheering him on.

Thank you, Daddy. Thank you for the gift of this boy, this child of my heart. Thank you for showing me how to love him, how to raise him, how to let him go. Thank you for being the North Star that guides us, the light that leads us home.

I love you, Daddy. I miss you. And I promise to keep shining your light, to keep walking in your footsteps, to keep loving with every beat of my heart.

Your little girl, always,

Remi

***

Dear Daddy,

The house is quiet now, the last of the guests gone home, the remnants of the celebration cleared away. And as I sit here in the stillness, my heart full to overflowing, I find myself marveling at the tapestry of our lives, at the way the threads of your love and your legacy have woven through every moment, every memory, every milestone along the way.

I think about the countless times I've felt your presence, your guidance, your love. The times when I was lost and afraid, when I didn't know which way to turn or what choice to make. The times when I closed my eyes and whispered your name, and felt your strength pour into me like a river, like a rush of grace.

I think about the way you've shaped me, the way you've molded me into the woman I am today. The way you taught me to dream big and love deep, to stand up for what's right and fight for what I believe in. The way you showed me that true strength comes from vulnerability, that true wisdom comes from humility, that true love comes from sacrifice.

And I think about the way you've lived on, the way your spirit has endured, long after you took your last breath. The way your laughter still echoes in the halls of my heart, the way your smile still lights up the darkest of my days. The way your love still guides me, still sustains me, still gives me the courage to face whatever lies ahead.

Oh, Daddy. There aren't enough words in the world to express the gratitude I feel, the love that swells inside me like a symphony, like a song of praise. There aren't enough ways to say thank you for the gift of your life, for the blessing of your love, for the legacy that will endure long after we're gone.

But I'll keep trying, Daddy. I'll keep saying it, keep living it, keep spreading it like wildfire wherever I go. I'll keep telling your stories, keep sharing your wisdom, keep passing on the lessons you taught me about faith and family and the power of a life well-lived.

I'll keep loving my babies the way you loved me, with a fierceness and a tenderness that knows no bounds. I'll keep supporting my husband the way you supported Mama, with a steadiness and a devotion that weathers every storm. I'll keep serving my community the way you served yours, with a heart for justice and a passion for change.

And I'll keep writing to you, Daddy. I'll keep pouring out my heart on these pages, keep sharing my joys and my sorrows, my triumphs and my fears. I'll keep seeking your guidance, keep leaning on your strength, keep basking in the warmth of your love.

Because that's what these letters have been, Daddy. A lifeline, a love letter, a living testament to the bond that even death could not break. They've been my way of keeping you close, of holding on to the parts of you that will never fade away. They've been my way of making sense of this beautiful, broken world, of finding my way through the wilderness of grief and into the light of hope.

And as I sign this last letter, as I close this chapter of my story and step into the next, I do so with a heart full of peace and a soul full of joy. Because I know that no matter what the future holds, no matter where this winding road may lead, I carry you with me, Daddy. In my heart, in my mind, in the very marrow of my bones.

I love you, Daddy. I miss you. And I thank you, for everything.

Your little girl, always and forever,

Remi

***

Dear Daddy,

It's a warm summer evening, and I'm sitting on the porch steps, watching the sun paint the sky in shades of orange and gold. Kwame is beside me, his head on my shoulder, his cap and gown folded neatly in his lap. And for a moment, it feels like time has stopped, like the world is holding its breath, waiting for the next chapter to begin.

We sit in silence for a while, just drinking in the peace of the moment, the sweetness of each other's company. And then, softly, Kwame begins to speak.

"Mama," he says, his voice thick with emotion, "I wish Grandpa was here. I wish he could have seen me graduate, could have been there to cheer me on."

I wrap my arm around his shoulders, pulling him close. "Oh, baby," I murmur, "he was there. He's always been there, watching over you, guiding your steps. And I know that today, he was bursting with pride, just like I am."

Kwame nods, a tear slipping down his cheek. "I know," he whispers. "I can feel him, Mama. I can feel his love, his strength, his spirit. It's like he's a part of me, like he's woven into my very soul."

I smile through my own tears, my heart aching with a bittersweet mix of joy and longing. "That's because he is, baby. He's a part of all of us, a thread in the tapestry of our family. And every time you love with your whole heart, every time you stand up for what's right, every time you chase your dreams with courage and conviction... that's him, shining through you."

Kwame is quiet for a moment, his gaze fixed on the horizon. And then he turns to me, his eyes shining with a wisdom beyond his years. "Mama," he says softly, "thank you. Thank you for keeping Grandpa's memory alive, for passing on his legacy, for showing me what it means to live a life of love and purpose. Thank you for being the rock of our family, the heart of our home. I don't know what I would do without you."

Oh, Daddy. In that moment, I feel a rush of love so fierce, so overwhelming, that it nearly takes my breath away. Because I see it now, with a clarity that pierces my very soul. I see the way our story, our legacy, our love, has come full circle. The way the seeds you planted, the dreams you nurtured, the promises you kept, have blossomed and borne fruit in the hearts of our children, and their children after them.

I see the way your spirit lives on, not just in me, but in every soul you touched, every life you changed, every heart you set ablaze with the fire of your love. I see the way your light shines on, a beacon of hope in a world that can be so dark, a reminder of the goodness and the grace that can be found in even the hardest of times.

And as the last rays of the sun dip below the horizon, as the stars begin to twinkle in the velvet sky, I feel a sense of peace wash over me, a knowing that settles deep in my bones. A knowing that no matter what the future holds, no matter where this winding road may lead, we will always have each other, and we will always have you.

I love you, Daddy. I miss you. And I thank you, for the life you lived, the love you gave, the legacy you left. Until we meet again.

Your little girl, now and always,

Remi

Afterword

Writing this book has been a journey of love, grief, and discovery. When I first set out to tell the story of Remi and her father, I had no idea how deeply it would resonate with my own life, my own experiences of loss and healing. Through Remi's voice, I found a way to express the complex tapestry of emotions that come with losing a beloved parent—the ache of absence, the comfort of cherished memories, the enduring power of a love that transcends death itself.

Remi's story is a testament to the resilience of the human spirit, to the way we find strength in the face of unimaginable heartbreak. It's a reminder that even in our darkest hours, we are never truly alone—that the love and wisdom of those who have gone before us can guide us, sustain us, and help us to build lives of meaning and purpose. In Remi's journey, I see echoes of my own path towards healing, towards learning to carry the legacy of my loved ones forward while also forging my own way in the world.

My hope is that this book will be a companion to all those walking the winding road of grief, a hand to hold in the darkness. May Remi's words be a balm to the brokenhearted, a reminder that even in the depths of sorrow, there is hope, there is light, there is love. May her story inspire us to cherish the precious bonds of family, to live each day with intention and gratitude, and to always, always keep the memory of our loved ones alive in the way we love, the way we live, the way we carry their legacies forward. And may we all find the courage to dance in the rain, to seek out the silver linings, and to trust in the promise of brighter days ahead.

About the author

Born and raised in Washington, D.C., I grew up surrounded by the country's capital's vibrant culture and diverse communities. My teenage years were spent in Maryland, where I sincerely appreciated the unique blend of urban and suburban life. From a young age, I was known for my shy and quiet demeanor, often finding solace in my thoughts and observations. This reflective nature led me to develop a keen interest in people, particularly in the wisdom and experiences of older adults. I spent countless hours in the company of elders, listening to their stories and learning from their perspectives. This early exposure to intergenerational interactions instilled in me a profound respect for the lessons that can be understood by those who have lived through different times. My journey took a significant turn when I joined the Army and served in Desert Storm. The experiences I gained during my military service were transformative, teaching me about resilience, teamwork, and the complexities of human nature. The discipline and perspective I acquired in the Army have been invaluable in shaping my worldview and approach to writing.